HAPPY TRAILS
TO YOU

JULIE HECHT

SIMON & SCHUSTER PAPERBACKS
NEW YORK   LONDON   TORONTO   SYDNEY

SIMON & SCHUSTER PAPERBACKS
A Division of Simon & Schuster, Inc.
1230 Avenue of the Americas
New York, NY 10020

First Simon & Schuster trade paperback edition June 2009

SIMON & SCHUSTER PAPERBACKS and colophon are registered trademarks of Simon & Schuster, Inc.

For information about special discounts for bulk purchases, please contact Simon & Schuster Special Sales at 1-866-506-1949 or business@simonandschuster.com.

The Simon & Schuster Speakers Bureau can bring authors to your live event. For more information or to book an event, contact the Simon & Schuster Speakers Bureau at 1-866-248-3049 or visit our website at www.simonspeakers.com.

Designed by Davina Mock-Maniscalco

Manufactured in the United States of America

10 9 8 7 6 5 4 3 2 1

The Library of Congress has cataloged the hardcover edition as follows:

Hecht, Julie.
Happy trails to you / Julie Hecht.
p.   cm.
Short stories.
Contents: Over there—Being and nothingness—A little present on this dark November day—Thank you for the mittens—Get money—Cramp bark—Happy trails to you.
I. Title.
PS3558.E29H37   2008
813'.54—dc22   2008007456

ISBN 978-1-4165-6425-6
ISBN 978-1-4165-6426-3 (pbk)
ISBN 978-1-4165-6617-5 (ebook)

In memory of my father and my mother,
David Hecht and Eva Shan,
and
Hattie Shan and Sam Martin
and Susan L. Meyer

CONTENTS

HAPPY TRAILS
TO YOU

OVER THERE

I OWED MY NEIGHBOR a visit. She'd left a message on my answering machine just before Christmas. It started with the words "All right, I'll leave a message . . ." People over eighty don't like answering machines, and I don't blame them. I'm like the Unabomber in that respect—hatred of technology. And also, as I heard him described on the news, "a follower of Thoreau."

The message was an invitation to come over and see the amaryllis I'd sent her, just bursting into bloom, but I ignored it. I knew she had a houseful of children and grandchildren, so I could postpone the visit. I figured, they're all in there eating their Christmas pudding, they don't need me. I'll go when she's alone with her dog and cat.

"All right, I'll leave a message" was something my father used to say when he accepted the answering machine after two decades. But I'm not going there, as I'd heard Geraldo say on his nightly "news" show. It's too sad for me over there.

A spiritual adviser was recently quoted as saying that most people have had their hearts broken by the time they're twenty, but he didn't say what had become of those hearts by age forty-five. My neighbor is almost ninety, about twice my age—also about twice as intelligent as anyone I know. The normal response would be to call her back. But she has a hearing problem, and on the phone she can't hear me. In person, I hoped that some lip-reading could go on.

Her sight hasn't failed her—she's luckier than my father was. Or her brain hasn't failed her, so the cataract operations can take place. In the case of my parent, mental confusion was used as a reason to prevent the cataract operations. But surely there's a solution to that. I should have made it my full-time job to find the solutions to all things at the time. Now that I know, it's too late. That's the secret of life—by the time you know, it's too late.

When I got the second message, I decided to go for a visit. I thought I should bring something, even though I'd already sent the double amaryllis in a clay pot with green moss, but a tin of organic cookies from a bakery in California wouldn't be appreciated over there. Besides, the red tin, to my surprise, had a poinsettia on the lid, and I'd tossed it into the recycling pail when I saw it.

A few days before, I'd baked a loaf of cranberry bread, but my husband had left it in the oven an extra hour. "I'm going for a walk," I'd told him. "Please check the bread when the timer goes off. If it's not done, set it for fifteen minutes more. Okay?"

Even though he was at his computer, he looked up and said okay. Anything to do with food will snap him out of it for a second. But when I returned from my walk—and Thoreau walked four hours a day, so I knew walking was a good thing to do even with a windchill of seventeen—I smelled the bread but saw no sign of it on the table or stove. "Where's the cranberry bread?" I asked.

"What cranberry bread?" my husband said.

I repeated the conversation we'd had. "I don't recall any conversation like that," he said.

The bread was dark brown, not black. So I carved and hacked it out of the Pyrex bread pan, even though it was pretty hot. "Get used to touching hot things with your bare hands," I remembered Julia Child saying on one of her TV shows. The reason given was that it saves time and is easier than grabbing pot holders.

The middle section of the bread was the least hard and burnt, and this was the section I planned to take to my neighbor. She's the one who gave me the recipe, but she doesn't approve of the results of my many attempts. For a few years, I baked the breads in a toaster oven because someone had cleaned our nineteen-thirties-era stove with oven cleaner and the toxic fumes lingered on.

As a pre-Christmas present to myself this year, and to celebrate my new series of photographs of people with their old appliances, I asked the Japanese cleaning helper if she would mind rinsing the oven with white vinegar and baking soda. In my early years of domestic servitude, in a manic spree, I cleaned our first oven and breathed Easy-Off fumes. My cleaning days are over, even though I buy only Ecover cleaning products, having heard on *All Things Considered* that the Ecover factory was the most ecologically advanced in the world. Employees were forbidden to smoke, even outside. I wanted to jump for joy when I heard that, but I was in the car, fastened in with a seat belt, so jumping was impossible.

The cleaning person agreed to my request. She likes the idea of cleaning with white vinegar, but not for the right reasons. It's almost impossible to teach ecology to immigrants. One problem is that they don't have the vocabulary for it. In my opinion, these words should be taught with their first English lesson. Words like toxic fumes.

"When I came to this country, I tried to buy vinegar for cooking and they gave me this," she said. "I tasted some, and I couldn't believe it!" Then we both started to laugh. "Is it true that some American people use this vinegar for salad?" she asked. I had to tell her the ugly truth. Then I'm expected to feel ashamed for the whole day, I suppose. I was reminded of the time I was told by a Japanese waitress that a kind of sushi made with fried tempura batter as an inner ingredient was invented just for Americans. "Because Americans like greasy stuff," she said.

During those early years, when cleaning an oven I often asked myself, "Would Jacqueline Kennedy be doing this?" Prin-

cess Diana was still a young teenager, so the comparison didn't
come up in her case.

I'll just grab the center section of the baked bread and bring
it with me to the neighbor's house, I thought as I spied some
red tissue paper that would look good over the tinfoil. Then I
found a flashlight and walked around the corner. As I ap-
proached the front door, I saw through the window a group of
people milling about. Because it was Christmas, they all must
have thought they had to wear red. Some were people I didn't
recognize, and from the Republican looks on their faces I
dreaded being introduced to them.

I thought I knew how to talk to normal Christians, even
though I had one Jewish ancestor—and they had one, too, if
they counted Jesus. I'd first tried to do this talk when I was six
or seven and my father left me in the toy department of Sears,
Roebuck while he went to the tool department. These were the
days before children were kidnapped from stores, and the toy
department wasn't far out of his sight. I was viewing the dolls
displayed on a shelf when I saw an extremely Catholic-looking
girl staring at a doll—she stared at it with an intensity I understood. At the time, I believed that all girls named Cathy or
Kathy were Catholic. Since it was November, I thought I should
say something I'd heard regular Americans say: "Are you hoping
to get that for Christmas?" But the girl turned on me and said angrily, "I'm getting it before Christmas! Whenever I want!"

A worse incident occurred the next summer when my father
brought me along to the tennis courts and I waited for him in

the shade while he played the game in the blazing sun. I was introduced to the daughter of my father's tennis partner, and we discussed our life stories for a while, getting to tonsillectomies, now known to be a bad mistake, tonsils being a first line of defense in the immune system. The girl said she'd had her surgery in a doctor's office and gone right home, and I said I'd been in a hospital in Manhattan and stayed a couple of days. The girl insisted that tonsillectomies were never done in hospitals, and she became furious. I couldn't interrupt my father at his favorite sport, and by the time it was over the girl had stormed off. I believe she even used the word "liar" in her final parting words.

When at last I got a chance to tell my father what had transpired he couldn't believe it. I wanted him to follow the other father and daughter and explain that the story was true, but they'd driven away. Where is this girl now? Probably in a psycho ward. Or, more likely, the head of a movie company in Los Angeles or New York. The one who has these events on the mind decades later is the one on the way to the ward. The two incidents with these girls were perfect preparation for life.

So I thought I knew how to behave among hard-core, everyday Christians, but still with a screaming inside. With this inner screaming going on, I walked into my neighbor's kitchen. Right away I smelled bacon. I kept this to my vegan self, though. Or, I should say, to myself and from that self at the same time. Just beneath consciousness, I might have assumed this: ham or bacon had been cooked there during the day.

"Merry Christmas!" people said as I walked in. I had made the faux pas of greeting a gang of people on the road earlier in the day by saying, "Hi." They quickly called back in a cold, indifferent, yet reprimanding way, "Merry Christmas!"

How should I remember it was Christmas when the temperature was up to sixty degrees again? At the time, circa 1997, no one took it seriously when I said the words "greenhouse effect" or "global warming." One man, an editor of my photo book said, "I love this caption: 'The world meltdown has begun.'" They all thought it was a joke. The weather was as dreary as it is in Beverly Hills at Christmas, or anytime, for that matter—the only good time in Southern California is when you're standing right under an orange tree.

When I got to my neighbor's house at six o'clock, they'd been saying "Merry Christmas" all day. They must be sick of it by now, too, I thought. Of course, they might not have known about my ancestor, the way the dermatologist I saw for sun damage didn't know either, when he used a special instrument to look into my irises and said, "You're a real WASP. Light hair, light skin, light eyes—you have to be careful."

My neighbor came over to me and said, "Merry Christmas." I smiled and leaned forward to give her a kiss. I had never given her a kiss before. I'd never gone over there on Christmas Day before. I'd always thought there was a formal religious meal going on until she told me that people just come and go all day.

"Sit down," she said. I sat down and she sat down in an easy chair across from me. Others were gathered around the table.

Then the introductions began. I showed them the cranberry bread and told the story. I summed it up. I've learned that people don't have much of an attention span.

"We use butter and eggs, but she brings over these macrobiotic treats for Mom," one of the daughters said. If only it were that easy to pass for macrobiotic.

I started off by smiling. I've discovered that smiling works better than talking. I have a new false smile that I use for occasions like these.

"You should have seen it here before," my neighbor said. "The people, the commotion! You would have hated it."

"I would have? How can you tell?"

"Instinct," she said.

On the night of this Christmas Day, my neighbor and I were dressed almost alike. Cotton sweatpants, old shirts, and running sneakers. "We want to be comfortable," she explained to the guests. For the special day, I had changed out of my flannel shirt and borrowed a corduroy shirt I'd bought for my husband a few years before. At the time, the shirt was moss-green, but an accident with Clorox had turned it beige. Not very festive.

How would she hear me with all the other talking going on was what I was worrying about. "Look at your amaryllis," she said. "It'll bloom in a few days."

"I told them not to put a bow in it!" I said as I pulled the red-and-gold ribbon out of the soil where it was stuck in with a tiny stake. "I told them, no plastic stake for the card. And they didn't use enough moss. I should have waited while they packed in the moss."

Suddenly the bottles appeared. Some requested wine, others whiskey. The moment of asking for bottled water was coming up. People don't like the one who asks for water. There's always the split second when they wonder if you're a former alcoholic. They can't imagine any other reason for declining alcohol. For example, it's a drug and it causes a drugged feeling.

I have to remember to bring my own water, I thought. Club soda in a soft plastic bottle is what they always had to offer. And here, on Christmas Day, not even that. I'd given my neighbor a copy of *Natural Health, Natural Medicine,* and she'd underlined almost everything in it. She loves Dr. Andrew Weil, even though he has a large beard and at first she thought he was a guru. But what about the sentence describing the seeping of the plastic into the water? "Soft plastic bottles can leach plastic molecules into the water." They can't take that in.

My neighbor's son handed me one of those bottles of water and a glass full of ice. I got up and threw the ice into the sink. "I don't need any ice," I explained to him. Another thing these people can't understand is not needing ice. Those who use no alcohol need no ice. "Ice is often contaminated by bacteria," I'd read.

The man seemed offended that I'd rejected the ice. In England, when my husband requested ice, he was told, "It's bad for the digestion." The real reason was that they didn't happen to have any. Only the greedy Americans requested ice water in

Europe at the time. Fortunately, we were driving a car with French license plates, so we brought no shame upon our country.

The only other beverage choice I saw at my neighbor's house was a spicy kind of V8, also in a plastic bottle. I checked the sodium count. It was around eight hundred. I should go home, I thought.

The regulars were pouring out whiskey for each other. A few ounces each, it looked like to me. In some Al-Anon literature I came across once, I'd read, "Don't count, don't watch the amount. It's not your problem." But that's not true. If you're there it is your problem. Then they had a motto: "You didn't cause it, you can't change it, you can't cure it," and some other useless claptrap for the person whose family member was addicted. It was like a bad little poem. The Al-Anon authors could have used some literary assistance.

"I have a joke for vegetarians," a red-faced man said after taking a gulp from his glass. I tried to prepare myself, but I'm never prepared for the people in our society. "If God didn't want us to eat animals, why did he make them out of meat?" he said proudly.

I pictured a cow. Then I pictured a deer, a duck, a rabbit. There was nothing I could say. I wanted to try a new version of my fake smile, a special version that would show how fake it is, but I couldn't.

"Oh," I said. They all went back to their merrymaking.

These people are confident. They don't need others to like

their jokes or their menu plans. They have their own lives, they're not worried about every sentence, and, most important of all, they have their bottles. The bottles were now on the table, right in the middle. I tried to get the gist of their conversation, but it wasn't exactly a conversation. There were no topics that I recognized. Global warming, asteroids crashing to earth—these subjects didn't come up. I thought I heard something to do with golf, but my brain doesn't process golf talk. Maybe this would be a good time to quote what Mark Twain said about golf—"A good walk spoiled." Probably not—golfers don't like to hear it.

"What is the purpose of a New Year's Eve party, or any kind of party, for that matter?" my father said when I was thirteen. Brilliant, Dad, I often say to him, wherever he is in the afterlife.

It turns out that he was right about most things. He disliked Christmas trees and celebrations of any kind. He might be pleased with the person I've become, but I'm not going there. That's forbidden territory, the land of wishing my father and mother were alive.

My neighbor and I made a few stabs at conversation but soon realized the futility of it. What is the etiquette when a person can't hear?

On one visit I tried writing things down after she said "What?" so many times.

"Who rakes your leaves?" was my question. Because the man who raked our leaves had a system of waiting until every last leaf was down. Did it occur to him to come to rake more than once?

I wrote his name down on a piece of scrap paper. "John Davis." Then I wrote, "Leaves." Then I wrote, "Lazy."

She got the picture. "'Leaves. Lazy. John Davis.' I like the way that looks," she said, smiling happily. I liked the way it looked, too. But I hoped John Davis wouldn't find the scrap of paper blowing around outside.

"HERE, TAKE some cake with you when you go," the daughter-in-law said to me as I got up. "Even though you won't eat it."

"She can give it to her husband," my neighbor said. How did she hear all that?

My voice is always blamed and given as the reason the deaf can't hear. I did once consult a deaf psychoanalyst who wore a hearing aid, and she rapped and tapped it angrily whenever I spoke. I guessed the idea was that you had to scream out your problems, even though it wasn't scream therapy or anything like that.

"Your voice is too soft," the referring doctor said when I told her what had happened. "I've never had any problem with her hearing," she added as a special touch. Typical.

The daughter-in-law was slicing a piece of cake and saying, "We covet this, so I'm giving you a small piece." The word "covet" was not correct, but instead of correcting her I said, "That's too big."

"Her husband can eat the cake," my neighbor said again.

I pictured my husband eating the cake for breakfast, as is his custom, when he sees any cake, and I pictured the ingredients and all the other ingredients he'd eaten in his life of forty-nine years—mayonnaise, pâté, eggs and bacon, chips fried in cotton-seed oil, roast beef, white bread, Jell-O—and I imagined myself alone without him. Then I imagined him as an invalid. Then I imagined something killing me before his habits killed him. I wished I could stop all the imagining.

My neighbor came over and opened up the sample of bread I'd brought. "It looks kind of dark and dry. You have to use a real oven," she said.

"She tries to bake this in a toaster oven," she explained to the group who didn't care about the subject. I wished I had some Xanax in my pocket.

"Try toasting it," I said in a loud voice.

"Oh, toasting it," she said. "I know that. I'm the one who started this whole thing, remember?"

"We put all those bad things in to keep it nice and moist," the daughter-in-law said.

"It's the oldness of the oven," I said. "I think I've mastered the texture with soy milk and ground flax seeds."

"It's the husband's fault," someone said. Then I heard what used to be called a guffaw.

"He needs more ginkgo!" the red-faced man shouted.

I must say, I was impressed that such a man was acquainted with ginkgo the brain-and-memory stimulant. On the other hand, health properties of ginkgo and garlic have been trickling down to the pharmacy level for quite some time. That's the real "trickle-down effect."

"More ginkgo for everyone," someone said.

"And less drinko," I said. I meant it. Alcohol affects the brain as well as the liver. I didn't bring up the Mark Twain sentence about golf.

"Right. Less drinko!" someone else said. Then the guffaw again.

"We have to take the ham out soon," my neighbor said to her children.

A ham had been baking in my presence. This was the reason I'd never asked to bake my cranberry bread in their oven. An Orthodox rabbi would have to give a million instructions before the oven could be used or a Buddhist monk might have an idea of what to do. I wished I could find a religion that combined Buddhism, Judaism, and the good parts of Christianity. I wished I could find something.

I'd been told that a stove could be sandblasted to be made fit for use by Orthodox Jews. The same must go for stoves for vegans. But I could never find a sandblaster to come and take our old stove apart. This had been the path to the use of the toaster oven. But how would my neighbor ever be able to hear all that?

★ ★ ★

I T WAS just a few days later that I got another call about the amaryllis blooming, again with the opening phrase, "All right, I'll leave a message." Before that, I'd gotten a message from her saying, "Here's my critique of the cranberry bread: Too heavy and undercooked inside. Come over when you can."

I tried the bread again. For this one, I used a timer—my husband was out of the picture for helping. When the bell rang, the bread was the right color and looked like the real thing.

My neighbor was alone except for the dog and cat. I could see her through the window. She was poking at a potato in the toaster oven. "Come in, come in, come in," she said. "Don't let the cat out."

I took off my jacket. Then I took off the pile lining. Then I took off my sweater and a shoulder pad fell out.

"What's that, a false bosom?" she said.

"Are you drunk?" I asked. "It's a false shoulder."

"Who cares about a big bust," she said.

"I'd rather have big shoulders," I said.

"They say when you get to middle age, the bust enlarges," she said.

"Oh, no! Why not the shoulders?"

"The Lord giveth, and the Lord taketh away," my neighbor said. This would be a good time to smile, I thought. It would be better than saying "Ick."

"Blessed be the name of the Lord," she said.

"Here, try this cranberry bread." I handed it to her.

"Let's see that," she said. "Oh, that's better. I can tell by the color."

My neighbor was lucky that her cataract surgery had been successful. Many old people are not so lucky. She could be even luckier if she'd get a hearing aid. But I wasn't going to tell her that. Even if I had, she wouldn't have been able to hear me.

I'd asked her children about it—we were in the same generation, I figured I could talk to them, in spite of the golf and the ham.

"That's the way she is, we can't change her" was what they said, or something like that. You could spend your whole life talking to the children of elderly people about how to help them. If only someone had told me some things to do to help my parents.

My neighbor had a helper for a while, but they didn't hit it off. That's often the case. "She couldn't even identify a robin," she told me. "I can't have someone like that around."

"I was going to leave you a message," she said. "'STOP TRYING TO BAKE BREAD. IT ISN'T WORKING.'"

"I think I have it down now," I said.

"Come on, let's sit in the living room. I've already missed *Jeopardy.*"

I followed her and sat down on the same sofa with her and the cat.

The cat was as big as a raccoon. I tried touching him. He

looked surprised, but I kept it up. I'd read that petting cats and dogs lowers humans' blood pressure. But my blood pressure is low enough. I hope my blood pressure doesn't get too low from the petting of the cat, I was thinking. It wouldn't be good if I keeled over in a faint.

We should get a cat, I thought. Or a dog. I'd like a few of each. I'd like pets—in their own houses, outside. I'd like parents, children, cousins, aunts, uncles. I'd like to be back in my childhood with all of these. I was allergic to cats, but I'd recently read that there's a way to make them hypoallergenic.

"He's getting fat," my neighbor said. "He gets no exercise."

That must be where the term "fat cat" came from. It had just occurred to me.

The cat stretched out in a crazy way. His midsection was huge. He looked like a cat pillow I'd seen in a toy catalogue. After the stretching was over, I tried touching his head. "Why are you doing this?" was his attitude. I got up and went over to sit on the other sofa so I could have a better view of the animal's face. I was thinking about touching his head again. Also, there was only one lamp on in the whole room, and I thought that if my neighbor could see my face the lip-reading could take place.

"Is it okay to put the light on?" I said.

"Why, do you like a lot of light?" she asked.

I felt as if we were in Poland during the Communist era, but the company was too privileged and the furniture too fine. On the bookcase next to the antique kerosene lamp I'd turned on, there were about fifty photos in frames. I'd always wanted to take a photo of these photographs. The people were all good-looking and seemed to be having fun. It wasn't a Communist-Poland atmosphere. They were skiing, dancing, graduating from Harvard. This is my neighbor's family. Sometimes she tells me the story connected with each photo. They're interesting stories.

Not that interesting. The year before, I had to stop looking at these pictures. It was too sad. Why aren't I part of a big happy family, I couldn't help wondering. I once heard a psychologist say, "Everyone wants to be part of a big happy family. At Christmastime, the feeling is more extreme."

Then the dog came in and looked at us. "The dog is as old and arthritic as I am," my neighbor said. "We're just padding around together, limping through the best we can. Aren't we, Jim?"

I felt like crying whenever I saw this dog. He had trouble walking and lurched around. This was why we didn't have a dog. As my father said when we tried to get him a dog, "No, thank you, I don't want to lose anyone else." I hadn't thought about that at the time. There were so many things I hadn't thought about. "You little fool!" I often said to myself later, the way actors say it to each other in movies from the thirties and forties.

" I SHOULD go home," I said in as loud a voice as I could. I got up and walked toward the kitchen. As a form of sign language, I reached for my jacket. It was an old green Barbour jacket, the kind Prince Charles wears on the Scottish moors.

"My nephew wears that for hunting," she said. "Men. Men and their fishing and their hunting and their boats." She shook her head. "They're cooking some ducks they shot. They skinned them pretty neatly, I hope," she added.

"I can't listen to that," I said as a hint. "I might faint."

"I just cook vegetables for myself nowadays," she said. "I'd never eat duck. Pretty rich, I imagine," she added with revulsion. "Do you ever eat a baked potato? You don't have to worry about starches."

"It's my face I have to worry about. This whole area is starting to go," I said, touching one of the worst areas.

"Look at mine," she said. "Age. The skin sags, the fat comes, the veins show." She touched her hands. The veins showed, but the hands looked good to me. She picked up a fork in one of those hands and tried to stick it into the potato on her plate. The potato skin was hard and I was afraid she might stab herself with the fork.

"Why don't you use a knife?" I said right into her hearing space.

"You're not supposed to use a knife on a baked potato!" she said.

There was always something to learn. I learned something every time I went over there.

"I'm not supposed to have butter, but at my age, what the hell," she said, digging out some butter with the fork.

"Why don't you use olive oil?" I asked.

"I'm not in the mood for olive oil, that's why! At my age, I can do what I want. Here, take a taste of this," she said, offering me a spoon.

I tried to get some potato without the butter, although I wished I could taste some butter now and then.

"The Chinese and Japanese don't use butter and they don't miss it," I said.

"You're American!" my neighbor shouted. "You can have a bit of butter now and then."

I tasted the potato. It was good. It was the best potato I'd ever tasted. I had to resist the urge to grab it and gobble it down, butter and all. Instead I reached into the pocket of my jacket, the horrible "game pocket," intended for ducks and other small animals, and I took out my Pellegrino bottle. I'd read about a model who said she drank water whenever she was hungry. Then I read a book called *Your Body's Many Cries for Water: You Are Not Sick, You Are Thirsty!* The book was my influence, not the model.

I walked over to the door. The cat was watching me. I could tell he wanted me to leave. The dog, too.

"Oh, wait, I want you to taste this," my neighbor said.

"Do I have to?" I said in a normal voice. Now, that's one advantage of talking to the deaf. You can say whatever you want. It would be just my luck that she'd hear that one sentence.

"I want you to see how sweet this is," she said. "It's the baked ham from Christmas."

"But I'm a vegetarian," I said. I didn't even yell. I wanted to yell or scream.

"I know, but this is better than most," she said. "It's not salty the way ham can be."

I pictured a pig I'd seen in a documentary about the high intelligence of pigs and the reasons people keep them as pets. One woman said she preferred the pig's company to that of her husband. In the era when men were called chauvinist pigs, it was actually an insult to pigs.

"I'm just having a little bit," she said, carving off some pieces. Then she took her plate and shuffled across the kitchen to an easy chair in the dining part of the room. She turned around and fell back into the chair. "There," she said as if she were surprised by the landing. The dog was asleep in front of her. The cat was gone.

"Do you want me to turn on CNN?" I asked in my loudest voice. This was before BBC was available, before CNN went the way of *Entertainment Tonight*.

"No, I hate television," she said. "I'm just going to sit here and have dinner."

I didn't see how she could sit and have dinner facing a doorway. No person, no PBS news, no book. What about feng shui was my other notion. I'd never seen either of my parents dining alone without reading. They had book holders to support the books in front of them.

At the beginning of the end for my father—though birth is really the beginning of the end—I arrived late for a visit with him. My father no longer understood the rush hour, and the fact that it would take me the whole day to get to his house by six o'clock. He'd started his dinner alone and was reading while dining. There was a small, cheap plastic radio I'd never seen before on the table in front of him. He was listening to an NPR news program. The sight of this radio and this book holder and this plate with only some white-colored fillet of fish and a slice of bread, without the colors of salad or vegetables—this broke my heart. But I didn't let myself know that my heart was broken. Instead I was annoyed.

My father could have had a snack and waited for me to make my arduous trip on the highway. A thoughtless idea on my part. That was the right time to have worked on him to move out to live near us. Right next door, or around the corner. He and my neighbor could have been friends. They both did crossword puzzles—I couldn't imagine why. Don't we have enough on our minds without trying to figure out which word fits where? When I brought up the subject of moving, my father said, "Let's wait and see how I age." But by the time you do see, the person can't be moved.

" THIS IS the way I have my dinner when the family is gone," my neighbor said.

"Well, okay," I said. Then I flashed her that fake smile I'd been using all the time. *"Bon appétit!"* I said.

She heard me, too. She smiled back. "Oh," she said. "As Julia Child used to say."

I'd forgotten all about that.

BEING AND NOTHINGNESS

I HAD A PANICKY feeling. Too panicky to do the breath-ing exercises recommended for anxiety by Dr. Andrew Weil in his recent newsletter, and every health-food store was sold out of kava in vegetarian capsules. I'd read in the news-letter that kava should be reserved for severe anxiety. It was the summer of 1998, and I thought the situation was right for kava.

All I wanted to do was lie down on the couch, where I'd be compelled to watch the many news shows about the investiga-tion of the President's personal life. Not that I was interested in this life—I couldn't believe that we lived in a world where such questions were asked. Each night, every hour, I hoped to hear that something had happened to put an end to it.

I'd recovered from the alarm of January, when I'd seen a TV reporter standing in front of the White House and saying, "FBI agents are fanning out all across the country." Why would they be fanning out over this, I wondered at the time.

In the beginning, the shows were a good distraction and helped me to stay on the treadmill for more than half an hour. I once got my heartbeat up to a dangerous level by going too far and too fast while watching *Geraldo* and CNN and another, even worse, cable network. But then it got to be the same story every day.

One night, I was just about to fall asleep when I heard Geraldo say, "Did she go to visit Betty or did she visit Bill?" This sounded like the plot from an old Archie comic book and startled me so that after laughing out loud for a second I was wide awake and had to watch another whole show to get near sleep again.

The head man on the next program had a voice more like a punishment and a torture than a human voice—you have to ask why a speech coach for the TV station didn't step in and take this fellow in hand. Still, he's not as low as another one on the worse network, the lowest one who doesn't have even seventh-grade grammar under his belt. This is our country now. I couldn't believe what I was hearing—to say nothing of the hairdos.

It would be bad to lie down on the couch and listen to all that over and over, I thought, because they're desperately scraping the bottom of the barrel, and when I watched and listened to the scraping, I knew that I would be wasting valuable moments of life. "Life is an ecstasy," said Ralph Waldo Emerson, and I agreed with him.

I was counting the days until the return of the psychiatrist I'd been consulting. I wanted to request one of the brief phone appointments we'd agreed on for the summer vacation, but every time I thought of the word "phone" I thought of the word "sex." Could we have a phone appointment? I wanted to ask, but feared the sentence would come out with the words "phone sex." And it wouldn't be a Freudian slip, it would be from having heard those words spoken over and over on the news. I also wanted to mention how shocking it was that descriptions of sex were on the front page of the *Times* and on all the newscasters' lips, but I knew I couldn't say the word "lips," either.

How will I bring up the topic without using any of the words necessary, I wondered. I didn't want to upset the psychiatrist, even though I knew that listening to this was part of his job. But his analysis was obviously a failure, and he remained a shy, stammering, befuddled person. Or else that was just an act he used to control people and get whatever he wanted.

I was referred to the doctor for the condition of severe anxiety. And this was before the summer. I should have breathed my way out of the anxiety, but I was already breathing and exercising so much that between the walking and the breathing and the treadmill I had scarcely a moment for anything except lying on the couch and watching the news. A vicious cycle would begin, not counting the news cycle.

The winter before, the lying on the couch would start with *Crossfire,* at 7:30 p.m., and I'd tell myself, I'll just watch this one program—then I'll turn it off and go back to work. I was trying to sort through hundreds of landscape photographs I'd taken in Nantucket for my next book. Many of these had the same exact subject in different light. But after *Crossfire,* I'd have to watch *World View.* Then, at nine, it would be time for *Geraldo,* with a quick switch over to *Burden of Proof,* at nine-thirty. My favorite of all the lawyers was Greta, but where did the Scientology fit in and allow her to think so clearly? Maybe the rumor of Scientology wasn't true. Then the ten o'clock *World View*—it would be the same as the eight, with new salacious details added between eight and ten.

At eleven, there would be no reason to watch the local news, other than waiting for the weather report. That was a relief—or maybe the History Channel would have Hitler's life story or the biography of some other Nazi. Rudolph Steinhardt was the handsomest man in the SS before he was disfigured by the burns caused by his fighter plane being shot down during the war. This was one of the facts I'd heard on the program. Before-and-after photos were shown of the once handsome SS man.

It was often Hitler week on the History Channel. There's always something new to learn about Hitler's early life—for example, that his feelings had been hurt by rejections from art schools, or that Wittgenstein insulted him once. Then, a quick break for David Letterman and back to the repeat of *World View* on CNN.

This second round was the one where the lying on the couch turned into sinking into and becoming one with the couch.

This was the time when the self with any sense of human dignity disappeared. After 1:00 a.m., it got to be too hard to get up and do the things necessary to go to sleep. I had to boil the water to dilute the teaspoon of valerian tincture—a double dose of valerian would be necessary. The condition couldn't be called tired—it wasn't awake, it wasn't asleep, it wasn't alive, it wasn't dead. After watching this cableful of shows, it was being and nothingness, it was the living dead.

Months later, with all this still going on, one day I noticed that it was the most beautiful summer day I'd ever seen. Probably I'd seen equally beautiful days, but had only recently come to understand Emerson's idea that the days are gods. But he and his friend Thoreau didn't have the special prosecutor ruining every day and night the way we did.

This particular day was really a god, and I'd wasted most of it in the new super-hot weather racing to flower farms, trying to get the last white annuals to add to the window boxes of our rented house in Nantucket.

If it had been our own house, I could have had the cable turned off. After I saw a bit of the *Geraldo* episode—the one with the discredited criminal detective explaining how to collect DNA with a Q-tip—that was the end—until the real end, when I saw an esteemed professor of law use the word "slobber." I couldn't believe the word. "Saliva," he said, then he said, "slobber," then, "from kissing." That was the end.

There was a time in America when we read about people throwing an ax through the TV screen, and this was just for the regular programs. Then there was the lucky Elvis Presley, who was reported to have used a gun to shoot out his TV screen when Robert Goulet was singing. But, one, I was in the rented house; and, two, I didn't have a gun handy. If I'd had a gun in hand, only a stun gun, and saw the special prosecutor, could I have controlled myself? He was the only person on earth with whom we couldn't shake hands—other than Charles Manson and various international killers. Every day people drop dead, but the prosecutor was evil, he was a chubette, yet he lived on, filmed daily with his black garbage bag in hand. "A rat, a roach, a snail has life," I thought, or "a dog, a horse, a rat . . . ," as King Lear said. Shakespeare must have had this kind of guy in mind.

This was the summer I had arranged to be in Nantucket long enough to photograph every pond, cloud, flower, and vine. But then came the doom-filled seventeen days in August—the days of waiting for the President to testify. I'd see him on the news, and he didn't seem concerned. "What, me worry?" was his attitude. Maybe he'd been influenced by *Mad* magazine as well as John F. Kennedy. This was before the real Alfred E. Neuman had been put into office as president.

During the first week of the seventeen days, I went to the organic-produce store every day. I remembered reading that the aroma of peaches had cured people of severe anxiety. This was right near the harbor and even when I didn't need any fruit or vegetables, I wanted to see the sailboats in the water and the white clouds in the blue sky. Also, this store was a good place to buy the *Times.* The newspapers were kept outside underneath a rock, in between pots of lavender. On one of those days, the owner asked, "What's wrong, are you worried about something?" He was tuned in to his organic-produce customers.

I had just seen Greta frowning when I checked out CNN. She had been forced to talk about DNA, and she said she was worried about what her mother would think.

"I can tell by your aura that something's wrong," the fruit manager said. I'd never heard her use the word "aura" before.

"I'm worried about the dress," I said.

"Nobody cares," the owner said.

"I'm worried that they'll use it to get him," I said.

"You'll see. Nothing will happen," he said with confidence as he put the *Times* into a bag of peaches.

I'd postponed buying the newspaper as long as I could, so the entire day wouldn't be ruined, but the afternoon still lay ahead. I'd tried to bargain with my husband to watch only CNN at night, but he informed me that CNN was the same as any other cable station. I was surprised to hear that. Didn't Jane Fonda have any influence while she was married to Ted Turner?

It was true that CNN's bearded correspondent, who used to stand outside the White House reporting the most serious world events, now stood outside every night and uttered the words "president," "affair with," "sex with," and then that name, which I couldn't bear to have pass through my mind. The correspondent seemed to have shrunk during these months and now he'd begun to resemble Toulouse-Lautrec.

At one time we were friends with a Republican, but it ended over political arguments. I'd said to him way back in January, after our first bitter fight, "We want to be friends, so let's agree never to discuss this again." But the Republican refused to agree, which was too bad, since he knew a lot about Beethoven and how the composer came to write the "Emperor" Concerto. I'd have to get musical tidbits elsewhere, I figured, when I saw into his right-wing soul. And to think, at one time we all went for nature walks together.

After the political argument, we managed to attend one more dinner at the Republican's home. His wife was a feminist and a liberal—the young and politically correct variety. How could this be? Even though the Republican was only forty-one, he was sitting in an easy chair with a glass of cognac in his hand. He had tried putting some Mozart on his stereo, but the guests weren't interested. Some were in the new generation that knows only the music of the last couple of decades.

I'd gotten a panicky feeling as soon as we'd arrived. I looked around the room checking for intellectuals, New York Jews, and homosexuals. There were none. It was a large room filled with Republicans and normal Americans. These people were the minority in the small town. They were acting overly polite and considerate, engaging in that empty small talk I'd seen in movies from the nineteen-fifties. "Would you like some more this or that?" "Wasn't it a nice day?" "We did some yard work." "We helped the minister with his lawn mower."

As I wandered from room to room, searching for a Buddhist, a Unitarian, a Democrat, a Quaker, a Shaker—anything—I came across some young women looking at a photograph of themselves from their college days. The girls had been piled up for the fun photo, all smiling and appearing to have nothing much on their minds but hairstyles and clothes. This was the beginning of the era of people taking photos of themselves for no reason. I stared at the photo and couldn't help saying, "You all look like M_____ L_____." That was the first and last time I said the name.

I PICTURED the faces of Patrick Buchanan and Greta Van Susteren while I paid for the peaches and the *Times* on that hot summer day of the seventeen days. Why must each day begin with the *Times*, I thought as I looked at the wretched headline.

"How many a man continues his daily paper because he cannot help it, as is the case with all vicious habits?" Thoreau said in 1854. "The mind may be made an arena for the affairs of the public, or a quarter of Heaven" was the other sentence of his that I had in mind. Nantucket was now down to only an eighth or sixteenth of heaven, especially in August. Range Rovers, trucks, mopeds, Rollerbladers, dishonest real estate brokers, and the development of the moors for houses had reduced it to this fraction.

The events of August had begun to heat up, along with the greenhouse weather, and, in addition to that, I was in a rented

house with a black kitchen—black sink, black leather-grain refrigerator—and two gigantic black TVs.

I couldn't believe it when I heard them begin to discuss the
dress. The psychiatrist was so lucky to have been in Tibet, but I
knew I'd have to mention it when he returned. He's the sort
who might have been visiting a Buddhist monastery.

When he did return, it turned out that he'd forgotten all
about the phone appointments. I should have been prepared for
that. But I was never prepared for his insane behavior. I started
with the panicky feeling. I didn't even ask how his trip was.
What was the correct etiquette in a case like this?

"But you missed the worst part," I said. "About the dress." I
immediately regretted it. The sound was excruciating—not
only the word "dress" but also the word "the." The two together were unbearable.

"The dress has gone away, I thought," he said in a casual way.
I guessed that he was reading another patient's chart.

"You don't know," I said. "Now it's back."

I had to remember that the man was never up on current
events. His reason was that he got home too late to watch
the news. You had to sympathize with him. What about the
11:00 p.m. BBC news? Too late for that, too, he said. Maybe you
had to envy him and sympathize with him at the same time.

Why did we have to talk about this? I had my own life
once—what was it? I couldn't remember.

"I can't talk about it," people would say, and then start right
in talking about it.

★ ★ ★

W HERE WILL it be worse to purchase the *Times,* I thought, as I tested the August heat to see whether to bike or drive. I pictured the coffee store where I'd have to see the fun-loving twenty-year-olds on the staff. Their whole lives were fun. I compared them to Nietzsche, whose biography I'd just read. "I have forty-three years behind me, but I'm as alone as when I was a child" was one quote. Then I pictured the people who frequented the organic-produce store—the yoga people, the Buddhists, the kava seekers, the Saint-John's-wort users.

This store declined to carry Dr. Weil's books, choosing *Eat Right 4 Your Type* and *Are You Getting Enlightened or Losing Your Mind?* Still, I decided to go there for the water view.

When I arrived, the fruit manager was juicing some dented fruit and talking about her failed romance. "How will I get along without him?" she asked, as if I might know.

"Maybe you can patch things up," I said.

"No, too much has gone on between Jim and I," she said with sadness.

"'Jim and me,'" I said. "Object of a preposition."

"Really? It sounds wrong. 'Jim and me.'"

"'Between Jim and me.' 'Between us,'" I said. "'Between them.'"

I remembered the host—if such a man could be called a "host"—of the cable show *Hardball,* saying, "A picture of my wife and I." Can you call in to these Republican supporters about their grammatical errors? One good thing about the President was his excellent grammar and his understanding of prepositions and the objective case. "Between Miss L_____ and me," I was happy to hear him say. But shouldn't it have been Ms.?

"Look," I said, searching for a paper napkin to write on—at least they had the ecologically correct, unbleached, tan kind. I grabbed it and wrote down a bunch of prepositions: "Between, of, for, to, about, from." Then I wrote down some objects. "Me, him, them, her."

"Didn't you diagram sentences in seventh grade?" I asked. "It was so much fun."

"Yeah, I guess we did, but it still doesn't sound right—'between Jim and me.'"

Then the fruit-juice girl held out a little tin labeled "Truly Organic Peppermints—Over One Hundred Mints Per Tin!"

Inside the tin was a starched-looking tissue paper neatly filled with small tan wafers. I could see something printed on the inside of the cover: THE MEASURE OF MENTAL HEALTH IS THE DISPOSITION TO FIND GOOD EVERYWHERE. —RALPH WALDO EMERSON.

I couldn't believe my good fortune. The quote influenced me to take one mint.

"When you've finished the other ninety-nine, would you save the tin for me?" I asked.

"Sure," she said. "Take it now."

She emptied the mints into a bag and gave me the tin.

* * *

MY HUSBAND and I agreed that the President's speech would be too painful to watch. Instead, we went for a walk around the hot, humid town. Other people were dining out, buying books, or walking around, the only three activities possible. But during our walk, I kept thinking about how the speech was going, the way it is when someone you know is having open-heart surgery.

When we got home, I called the bookstore to order a book about Nietzsche's last days. Reading that would be better than watching the news. The manager answered and said he was busy listening to a friend describe the speech.

"He reports that the President did well," he said.

I flicked on the TV with the remote.

"You'll be sorry," my husband said.

"Oh no, that witch is on," I said into the phone.

"Which one?" the manager asked. He knew the whole cast of the right wing and was a fan of *The Nation*.

"Buchanan's sister."

"Oh, that one," he said, as if the thought of these people had immediately depressed him.

THE PSYCHIATRIST hadn't heard about the speech. In fact, once again, he'd forgotten about the appointment itself.

"I haven't had a moment! I have too many patients in the hospital, I'm simply run ragged!" he said in a desperate way. I pictured people going crazy from the investigation of the President's personal life and the broadcasting of it day and night.

I dreaded being put in the mental ward of the doctor's hospital, or even a better place like the former McLean's, where Ralph Waldo Emerson's brother had been treated. I tried everything Dr. Andrew Weil recommended—kava, Saint-John's-wort, breathing, walking, yoga.

The psychiatrist knew nothing about feng shui, and hadn't even heard that light pink was good for calming psychoses and that it was used in padded cells. "You're making that up!" he'd said in his mad way when I mentioned it.

All summer, I'd been trying to read the biography *Emerson: The Mind on Fire.* I'd ordered the book after reading *Thoreau: A Life of the Mind.* Even though I quickly forgot everything in that book, I thought I'd like to pack my brain with knowledge from this new one. Then I'd go back and reread *A Life of the Mind* before I forgot what was in *The Mind on Fire.* In that way, I'd be able to have all the information in my head at once.

Where could I fit in Nietzsche's life story? That would be difficult. To the authors of biographies, I wanted to say: "Too many facts, in no particular order, can be hard to take in."

When I saw the picture of Emerson on the cover I wanted to have the book. The expression on his face was an expression I'd never seen on any other face. Compare this face with the faces of Patrick Buchanan, Orrin Hatch, and Jerry Falwell.

After reading here and there all over the book, feeling too inferior to Emerson and the other transcendentalists to keep going, I put the book on a chair next to the bed where I could always see the picture. After a while, the weather got so hot that I had to close the window and turn on the air conditioner, but the window wouldn't stay closed. The one book heavy enough to weigh it down was *The Mind on Fire,* spine down.

Only on nights when it cooled off could I remove the book, let the window pop open, and have a chance to read it. After the heat became permanent, I gave up and left the book on the window. I had to look at Emerson's face sideways for the rest of our time in the house with the black kitchen.

Soon after the speech, we moved into another rented house with a light-pink kitchen. The long white counter had room for many bottles of vitamins and space left over to chop vegetables. When had I last chopped any? We went out every night to avoid turning on the TV. Even in the hip luncheonette-turned-restaurant, I heard the news being discussed. Nantucket was like a college town without a college.

THE AUTUMN clematis was blooming way ahead of past years, due to global warming—another reason why they wanted to destroy the President, for allowing the Vice President to bring up that subject.

I had expected to see the usual article about clematis vines in the local newspaper, but while I was looking for it, to my dismay, I discovered a special quiz asking whether the President should be removed from office. Since all nine respondents said no, I became more sure in my resolve to move to Nantucket someday soon. There, or Italy. I'd read that only in Italy had Nietzsche found peace of mind.

"There is indeed a great emptiness around me. Literally there is no one who could understand my situation," he wrote. I'd read this in *The New York Review of Books* in July, as I crossed the sound by ferry from a dental appointment in Hyannis back to Nantucket at night in a thick fog. I'd dug my emergency cell phone out of my canvas camera bag and left a message for my husband at his office in Boston: "I'm on the ferry in a dense fog."

I compared my situation to that of the philosopher, and right then got the idea for a title for my next series of photographs: "No Cell Phone for Nietzsche."

I'M ALL alone, I thought, just like the philosopher. There was no one to understand my situation. I wished that Greta Van Susteren were my friend. It was the middle of the night and most of my friends were asleep. I had only one subject to talk about. I thought of a close friend who would be awake, but she didn't have cable TV in northern Maine and didn't know how the Supreme Court worked. The most spiteful right-wing Republicans weren't on her list of people she'd like to slap in the face.

The day the Report came out, I decided not to read any part of the *Times*. "It is important to preserve the mind's chastity," Thoreau said.

The special prosecutor had begun to remind me of Liberace—the voice, the smile, the tone. The editorials were forbidden territory, too—they were like editorials in a high-school newspaper. Even the weather page felt bad to the touch. Every page was tainted.

"Thoreau would have the mind feed upon the works of nature, and not trouble itself about the news." I was thinking of this quote as I decided not to watch the President's testimony. "Think about your own problems," my husband said. "Try to get your royalty statement," he added with insensitivity.

THE NEXT afternoon, my yoga teacher came by to give me a lesson. The lesson was in exchange for photographs I had taken of her doing yoga with her cat. She stepped up onto the porch, threw her yoga mat onto the floor, and started to unbutton her shorts. The teacher and I had become friends. The friendship was based on discussions of veganism, vitamins, and our sympathy for the President, even though she tried to get me to stand on my head and once asked, "Have you ever taken LSD?" She was a wild thing, as in the song "Wild Thing," by Jimi Hendrix, the way she stood outside on the porch pulling her shorts off and putting on her yoga pants. There were no neighbors around to see her quick change, and the porch was surrounded by branches with leaves and hydrangeas still in bloom. All in one smooth movement that must have come from years of yoga and dance, she threw down the mat, unbuttoned her shorts, and pulled them off as she said, "I looked up 'sexual relations' in the dictionary, and he's right about the definition."

"Absolutely. But why does the whole world have to think about the definition?" I said.

"Did you look it up?" she asked.

If only she hadn't been standing there in her white underpants as she asked this.

"I couldn't bear to read any of it," I said

We could have been talking about the lives of Thoreau and Emerson. During our second exchange, she mentioned that the Nantucket Atheneum Library had copies of lectures by our two idols—Thoreau and Emerson, not our other two idols, Elvis Presley and President Kennedy.

"You can go to the Great Hall and stand where they stood," she told me. "You can pick up their vibes."

At one time, I didn't care much for the President and neither did the yoga teacher. We both voted for Ralph Nader, after we were sure that the Republicans were losing. To think I used to complain about the blow-drying of the President's hair.

"I admire his strength of character," she said, pulling on the yoga pants.

"I do, too. The worst thing he's done is to drink Diet Coke during the televised testimony."

"Or any kind of Coke," she said.

★ ★ ★

I t w a s the hour for *Crossfire*, but I decided not to watch unless Michael Kinsley was on.

"Well, you *did* come on this show, and we *are* talking about it," he'd recently said to a Republican who tried to pretend he was above discussing something.

Instead, I went upstairs to check the last light of the day on the open field outside the house. "Beauty had made Emerson its slave many a time," I'd read. This was the same kind of slavery.

On my way, I noticed from the hall window that the American flag was flapping around in the wind. I'm patriotic, but why do people hang the flag outside? All of a sudden, I couldn't stand looking at the flag and hearing it flap around anymore. Some nights, the flapping kept me awake, but I dreaded asking the psychiatrist to refill the emergency sleeping prescription, because even though he was only fifty-eight, the last time I'd asked, he had no recollection of what the drug was, or that he'd ever prescribed it.

On an evening like this, I thought, the best solution is to take down the flag. It's the patriotic thing to do. Because when people see the flag, they're reminded of America—our country—and what's going on inside it. It's not like burning the flag. If asked about it by a neighbor, I could blame it on the wind—a breeze was always blowing in Nantucket before global warming kicked in.

I brought the flag inside. Then I decided to lie down. I was all tired out from pulling on the flagpole. The view through the window was even better without the red stripes. While I was looking at the field, the sky, the clematis blossoms, and the way the tiny white petals were covering the fence, I knew that whatever they were saying on *Crossfire,* I didn't care anymore.

If I turned it on to check, my mind would be instantly besmirched by the opening salvos. What kind of human being could be a right-wing Republican? I was thinking about our former friend. How could he have Beethoven's life story in his head, along with the music of the "Emperor" Concerto, and support the prosecution of the President?

Even though I'm not psychic, I knew that the defense on the left wasn't strong enough. Why did they keep saying "deplorable conduct"? There were no grounds for comparison—no investigations of the other politicians' personal lives. One thing we did know—the investigation was the crime.

I thought I might be starting to like the President more than ever. Or else, I loved him like a brother. Certainly I admired him more. We were in the same generation, though I was the only one in our generation who'd never smoked marijuana.

We had things in common. We loved Elvis Presley, and then John F. Kennedy. I wished I could be more like Hillary—or even a little bit like her. I wished she could be a little like me, with the yoga and the botanical remedies. I bet she could have used some kava right then, but if word got out that they used herbal remedies, another investigation could start.

I'd wasted most of the summer thinking about all this while I walked the same lanes Emerson and Thoreau had walked. I stood right on the podium in the Nantucket Atheneum Library, where they both had spoken, but I was in such a hurry to get back outside into the godlike day that I tripped on my way down. The truth was that I was rushing off the podium because I felt unworthy to stand where they stood after the news I'd watched and read.

As I looked out at the field and the clouds and the sky, I remembered how much I loved Massachusetts—more than any other state. And I loved America, too. It was better than Pakistan. And I loved the American flag, even though it had those bright-red stripes clashing with the pale pink and white flowers in the window boxes—I hoped no one would notice that it was missing. And if people did notice, I hoped they would believe my reason for taking it down.

"EVERY THOUGHT WHICH PASSES THROUGH THE MIND HELPS TO WEAR AND TEAR IT."

I had picked up the vibes.

A LITTLE PRESENT

ON THIS DARK NOVEMBER DAY

I T STARTED WITH THE goldenseal powder. I saw the waiter in the all-night supermarket, where he was looking for a remedy for a sore throat. The all-night schedule had been changed. The supermarket now had to close at 1:00 a.m. because of its proximity to several bars. The bars closed at that hour, letting out young drunkards who liked to roam the market in search of more alcoholic beverages, cakes, and candy.

In the beginning of this era of bad behavior, the Nantucket police were posted inside and outside of the market. Not a squadron of police, or even a squad, just one policeman inside and one outside. But, as the manager explained to me, there was too much serious trouble for the police to control. Not only aimless violence, like fights and general wildness—the young drunkards would knock over shelves of merchandise just for fun.

"You can come in," the manager had said to me on the occasion of my first visit to the store after the new 1:00 a.m. closing had been put into place. That was when he told me the reasoning behind the decision.

But our schedule kept me busy until twelve-thirty or one. After waiting until dark to dine—and dark was 9:00 p.m. in late June and early July—we walked around the town of brick sidewalks and antique houses and then went to the bookstore. We rushed home to watch *The Daily Show*, preferring the fake news to the really fake real news. Then, if David Letterman wasn't on vacation, we watched his show, skipping the part where Hollywood actors were interviewed.

The Weather Channel and these two programs were the only programs left for me to watch on TV. A&E *Biography* was hit or miss. You couldn't count on them to pop up with Janis Joplin. They might have Dick Van Dyke or Lawrence Welk.

THE WAITER was the kind of waiter who was an actor, and he looked like an actor or a surfer. He was physically fit to an extreme degree, with the kind of muscles in his arms that many people in today's world—the new junk world of America— strive to have. His long, thick platinum-blond hair and overly tanned skin added to his California surfer-boy look.

I had spoken to him about the evils of suntanning to no avail. He had his reasons, and he said that his method of super-tanning was to add instant tanning lotion to sunscreen. When he explained this, I had to give up.

Among the waiter-actor's other physical attributes were his exceptionally well-formed and very white teeth. White teeth are now within reach of almost everyone. When I remark on the whiteness of the teeth of someone I know well enough for this kind of discussion, the person says, "I bleached them with trays from the dentist," or "I used White Strips from the drugstore." The bleaching method used now has a more natural result than the old Hollywood capping style.

A good example of this was the case of the angry Republican on the TV show *Capital Gang.* During the years of watching this program, I noticed that his teeth were too discolored for his TV job. Then, as if the producers of the show were mind readers, one night he showed up with bright-white caps, the whiteness blasting out from his sallow-skinned, miserable so-called face. The new bleaching technology must not have been ready in time for him.

As for John Kerry, he should have known better, or, as is his style, been advised better. He could have spent an hour in the dental chair, with the expensive light-bleaching procedure, instead of whatever super-white technique was done, since his campaign got revved up in the tooth department later on, just in time for those whitening lights, or whenever all that started in. One is loath to remember when pictures of all the Democratic candidates were shown on *The Daily Show* as a joke. What was the joke? Who was the most boring and dull, that kind of joke.

The waiter had told me that he'd used the bleaching trays, but with a special natural aloe-and-lemon-juice bleach. The ingredients had a fraudulent sound. He promised he'd find out the name, but was so busy working six days and nights all summer that I never asked again.

Other information the waiter had been willing to share with me was the name of the person who lightened his thick blond hair to the tone of surfer-lifeguard blond. I told him how a high-lighting accident had turned a section of my hair bright orange and gold, instead of the platinum-beige he and I both favored. "That's happened to me, too," he said with deep empathy. "It had to be corrected. It cost a fortune."

The waiter always dressed in a spiffy, well-pressed shirt—or maybe it was just that his wide shoulders, narrow waist, and excellent muscle tone made any shirt look extra good.

It was a surprise to see the waiter looking wan and bedraggled as he searched the pharmacy aisle for cold remedies. He said it wasn't just a cold; it was his throat. "It feels like there's something tied around my neck, choking me." He demonstrated by putting his large hands around his neck to choke himself.

The waiter had the voice of a great actor—Alec Guinness

or Laurence Olivier—and the elocution to go with it. Anything he said sounded interesting and worth the time invested listening.

It's never fun to look for herbal remedies in the supermarket's vitamin section—the unknown brands, the big corporations trying to cash in on the natural-remedy fervor, the strange and incorrect combinations of ingredients—but I wanted to help the waiter cure his sore throat by directing him to gargle with goldenseal powder dissolved in salt water. This remedy is ignored by millions who think they should ingest goldenseal for colds. Whenever I've influenced anyone to use the formula, which is mentioned repeatedly in Dr. Andrew Weil's writings, the person reports a magical, overnight cure. These people are hard-core skeptics and/or ignoramuses, too.

When we couldn't find the goldenseal powder, we looked for slippery elm tablets and echinacea tincture, but after walking up and down and back and forth under the cruel fluorescent lighting, we found none of the remedies. The waiter said he'd go to the health-food store the next day.

Even though Nantucket is a small town, or island, I was surprised to see him the very next day at the health-food store. He was in his beach attire—shorts and one of his jazzy, fitted, open-chest shirts—this one turquoise blue.

"I'm here," he said when he saw me. "Can you help me find the remedies?" He said this in the most polite way.

"It will take one minute," I said.

I didn't want the manager to get hold of him and tell him to

drink goldenseal tincture. Clerks in health-food stores are allowed to say whatever they want, without having any knowledge or correct information. In several European countries,
clerks who recommend vitamins and herbal remedies are required to be trained the way pharmacists are, and only then are
they permitted to make recommendations.

I showed him the cramped aisle and confusing shelves where
the tinctures and powders were kept, and he found the ones he
needed.

I WAS used to seeing the waiter at work in the diner-
luncheonette restaurant where four-star, low-priced dinners
were prepared by two iron-men chefs right behind the counter.
There was no air-conditioning or any air for the chefs, but several open windows, doors, and fans kept the air circulating for
the diners.

The waiter never seemed to be waiting tables; he seemed
more like an actor in a play or movie, a dancer in a ballet, or a
model on a runway, with the plates as props overwhelmed by
his large frame and startling appearance.

When he took orders, he seemed to be listening to an important confidence. Because he was so tall, he had to lean over, and
because the small restaurant was always filled with diners,
laughing and talking, pouring out the alcohol from bottles
they'd brought in, he had to lean over with his head right near

the person ordering. This contributed to the impression of his listening to something much more serious than a food order.

THE MENU was just the right length. Not that I read the menu—I dismissed most of it, searching quickly for whatever vegetarian possibilities might be drummed up. The chef was willing to deconstruct his menu for any kind of special order—"Salmon, no salmon," they called it in their hip style when someone ordered only the vegetable part of the plate. Although the chef would never use tofu unless it was part of an Asian recipe, he kept some in the refrigerator, and he would use it to replace the animal protein in any choice on the menu.

When I saw him cooking the tofu, using the grill on which he cooked parts of various animals, I asked him whether he would cook it in a pan. He always had six pans going at a time, and a vegan yoga instructor had told me that she asked him to use a pan when she ordered tofu. This gave me the courage to make the request.

"Don't worry, I always cook yours on a virgin part of the grill," the chef said.

I'd spent years watching him throw things on the grill and I knew that there was no such part.

Sometimes the waiter would have to kneel down to hear the order, and this never seemed right, for some to be sitting and dining while others were kneeling and serving.

He was so tuned in to the vegetarian orders that he would suggest and remind us of something we hadn't noticed on the menu. I'd be grateful to find two vegetables or one vegetable or one bean and brown rice, but the waiter wouldn't think that was good enough. He would offer: "How about some arugula pesto?" or "We have the fresh garbanzo beans—we shelled them today." He had a tone of supplication when he made these offers.

THE ONLY day the restaurant closed was Sunday and everyone in town except John Kerry knew this. One of the restaurant's two owners told us that the presidential candidate would leave messages on their machine.

There were only two tables outside, but these were the only tables where a group of people could talk and hear each other.

She did an imitation of his voice: "Hi, it's John Kerry. Could we get a table for six outside on Sunday night?" His calling in the request was no big deal to her.

"You mean he calls himself?" I asked. "Doesn't he have an assistant for that?"

"He's always called," she said. "He wants to come for dinner on Sunday, but he forgets that we're closed."

Both the hipster-chef and his beautiful-looking co-owner were supporters of the candidate. Still, they saw no connection between their fervent wish to defeat the Alfred E. Neuman president and their need for a day off.

"He must have other things on his mind," I said.

"Of course," she said.

"You could stay open for him," I said.

"The chef wouldn't want to," she said.

"What if he were President, would you stay open for him then?" I asked.

She thought for a second and shook her head. "No, the chef wouldn't want to," she said. Behind her lovely poker face there must have been a long story about this.

Why would John Kerry want to dine on the patio? It wasn't even a patio, but the end of a dark, narrow alley that opened up into this tiny courtyard, where there were two old wooden picnic tables. There were some big pots of white flowers, but the view was of the area where the sous-chef was working on micro-green salads.

In the opposite direction, facing out, there was a view of the back windows of houses where it would be impossible for the Secret Service to prevent snipers from hiding.

AFTER WE left the health-food store, the waiter and I stood outside in the small sand-and-dirt parking area across from the harbor. I could see the sailboats under the blue sky as we discussed his predicament. The colors of the sky and the water made almost any discussion seem pleasant. I was grateful to be in such a parking area rather than in an asphalt parking lot on a busy corner or on a plain sidewalk in a regular town. Only the blazing sun of the not-yet-believed global meltdown was a distraction from the setting—the sun and also the waiter's situation.

"Can't someone fill in for you tonight?" I asked.

"No, we're short-staffed," he said. "I have to go home, take these tinctures, do the gargle, then shower, get dressed, and be at work by two o'clock."

"Two o'clock?" I said. I had imagined that the waiters arrived ten minutes before the restaurant opened for dinner at six, the way certain people who watched David Letterman's show thought he arrived for work ten minutes before the show began. I had heard the TV host make annoyed reference to this lack of common sense.

"Yes, two o'clock. I have to prepare. I have to dry every plate, fold every napkin, polish every glass."

"I didn't know the waiters did that," I said ignorantly, with increasing sympathy. It wasn't these chores, it was the being indoors from 2:00 p.m. until midnight, doing kitchen work.

"It's only once a week," he said. "We take turns doing the preparation, but today is my turn."

I WAS surprised to see the waiter at the restaurant the next night. He appeared to have made a complete recovery. He was racing around the small space, so I wasn't able to ask him about his throat until we'd been seated.

"I'm almost cured," he said. "Thank you for the remedies. They really worked."

I didn't want to take credit for quoting a paragraph I'd read in a book, but since people don't like to read anymore—even one sentence is too much for them—maybe this kind of help is of some value. Reading, listening, and thinking have all fallen out of favor, gone by the wayside, especially with the new generation to which this fellow belonged.

I thought I was too young to be referring to anyone as part of the new generation. Because my generation was there, preteen, for the beginning of rock and roll and Elvis Presley, I believed we were the new, young generation and that this was a permanent state.

The next time I saw the waiter at the restaurant, I was sitting with a friend at the counter. My husband had left to return to his work on the mainland, or America, as it was called by many residents of Nantucket. I was now free to discuss botanical medicine however the circumstances dictated, and the circumstances were always dictating.

I asked the waiter how he was and he said, "I'm cured." Then he stopped for a second and said, "Are you finished eating?" He glanced at our plates.

We said yes to the waiter's question. I was afraid of what the next subject would be, following his odd query. "May I take your plates?" had always been the rule.

"There's one thing," the waiter said. "It's not that bad—but I wouldn't want to discuss any kind of symptom while people are having dinner." He had that beseeching, apologetic, supplicating tone going.

Then he leaned forward, still holding two salad plates in his hands, and said, "It's just that my tongue hurts. Is that weird?"

I had never heard of the symptom, although I had heard of burnt mouths, caused by chili peppers, leading to painful mouth ulcers. I told the waiter about those and he said, "I knew it was too good to be true to get better so fast. It must have just moved or settled in."

I was under pressure to come up with a remedy, but having no medical knowledge, and only the pages on minor ailments memorized from Dr. Weil's book, I was stumped.

"It's probably nothing," I said. It was a sentence I'd heard other people say. "But I'll look it up when I get home."

W HEN I got home, just in time for *The Daily Show,* I looked through the book of remedies. Then, unable to fight off the need to tell the waiter what I'd found out, I called the restaurant. There was a rerun of the show on, so I didn't have to watch it.

The sous-chef answered. I could hear him scrubbing the stove with industrial-strength Brillo. I asked for the waiter. He'd just left. Even knowing how crazy it sounded, I couldn't stop myself from saying, "Could you call him on his cell phone and give him a message?"

I knew he had a cell phone, a tiny silver one that lit up blue in all the important areas. He'd once lent it to me to make a call, and when I tried to get one from AT&T, the cost was prohibitive. Members of his generation always have the great deals on cell phones.

"I don't have his number," the sous-chef said. "But I'll give him a message when I see him."

"Okay," I said. "Tell him to gargle with goldenseal powder. I saw the remedy in Dr. Weil's book."

The sous-chef repeated the message aloud for the benefit of the head chef and other staff. "He has to gargle with goldenseal." Then he asked me, "What's it for?"

"He recovered from the sore throat, but his tongue hurts," I said.

The sous-chef was laughing as he called out again to the chef, "His tongue hurts."

I could hear them all laughing together as they cleaned and scrubbed and swept, and set out small-sized bottles of Heinz ketchup on the tables for the next day's breakfast.

"I'd like to see that book," the sous-chef said. "And your last book of photos. The one with the former sous-chef."

In addition to the book of remedies, I had a copy of *Eating Right for Optimum Health* I'd ordered for the chef—not that he was interested in either part of the title.

I wanted him to read the short list of healthful oils: olive and organically produced canola. The list of bad oils and reasons behind the badness was a long list.

He'd told that me his favorite dish at a nearby restaurant was "calves' brains on toast points." When I laughed at the words—

a laugh of horror mixed with admiration for his wit—he said, "It's not a joke. It's on the menu, I'm serious."

THE CHEF'S partner had a style she'd devised herself without trying. She was like Catherine Deneuve in the movie where the actress plays the role of a woman running a theater during World War II—business and beauty combined in her style—stockings and garter belts, too. I tried to hand her the books I'd brought for both chefs and she said, "The boys are outside; you can deliver them personally." It was the hour for her to count the money and check on various business matters.

I went around and looked into the alley where the two chefs liked to drink beer and wine and also to smoke cigarettes before cleaning up the cooking area. But now the alley was empty. Other times, only their lit cigarette tips and white chef's shirts were visible in the darkness.

I walked back through the restaurant. Outside the kitchen door, I could see the two chefs sitting and smoking at the picnic tables.

"Come out and sit down," the chef called to me. "We're ordering for the weekend. Sit there, upwind from the smoke."

I gave him the books and he took a quick, uninterested glance.

"Is this where John Kerry sat?" I asked as I sat down.

"No, he always sits here," the chef said. "Where I am."

"If he sat here, he'd have to look at that door," I said looking up at a chipped, painted wooden door with a rusting pad-lock.

"He doesn't care," the chef said. "He loves it out here. He wants to face the kitchen. The Secret Service wouldn't let him face away from the entrance anyway." Then he added, "they want their clients to be shot at from the front." He laughed his wild laugh.

I sat down.

"Four years ago when I sat out here, the former sous-chef said he had just cooked dinner for John Kerry. He said, 'John is going to be president someday.'"

"What was his dinner?" both chefs asked at the same time.

"Salmon with vegetables," I said.

The chefs looked disappointed. Their secret sauces hadn't been needed.

The hostess-owner floated out onto the patio.

"He's always come in here," the chef said. "He'll sit at the counter and discuss the Red Sox. He'll stand and talk in the dish room while we clean up. And now it's, 'What did he eat?' 'Where did he sit?'" Then the chef put his head in his hands and rubbed his eyes. I thought he might start to cry.

In all the summers I'd seen him standing behind six pans for four hours in over-one-hundred-degree heat, I'd never seen him put his head in his hands. He did once say, "Kill me, please, someone kill me."

"First came the Secret Service," he said. "I kept sautéing my vegetables as if I had nothing more important to do than look down at the sauté pan. Then he came and shook my hand at the counter. I said, 'I hate when you come in here because it takes the attention from me.' He just laughed."

"I didn't know he could laugh," I said. "I hope you washed your hands before stacking up the arugula. Because of all the hands he shook before he got to yours."

"Germs make the salad better," the chef said.

"His face was this close to mine—one inch," the sous-chef said. He demonstrated the distance with his fingers.

"You should have kissed him," I said.

"I wanted to! I said to everyone, 'I wanted to kiss him!' Wouldn't it have been great?"

He burst into laughter as only a twenty-five-year-old man can burst into things.

"He definitely had his chin worked on," a waitress said. She had come out to join the fun. "He used to have a smaller chin."

"Gigantic chins run in his family," I said. "Remember the photos of him testifying before Congress in 1973?"

"No. It's just that now he has a normal chin," she said.

"I was told that he had elephant-man disease in the form that causes the chin, hands, and feet to grow," I said. "The cure is to laser the pituitary gland to arrest the growing. Then plastic surgeons remove the excess jawline."

"Then why was his chin smaller when he used to come in here for dinner?" the waitress asked.

"They must have taken off too much," I said. "Then, next surgery, they added some back on. That's the only explanation."

"It makes sense," the hostess-owner said.

"Do you mind if we do the order?" the sous-chef asked me.

"I should leave."

"No, we come out here and talk and smoke and drink every night," the chef said. "It's depraved, isn't it?"

"We need to relax any way we can," the sous-chef said. "We cooked dinner for the next president."

"When he wins, the whole world will breathe a giant sigh of relief," the chef said.

"But what if the other thing happens?" I said.

"We don't think that way—he has to win."

"Someone on our corner had a 'Veterans Against Kerry' sign," I said.

"I hope you ripped it off," the chef said.

"Of course, I said."

It must have been a violation of the historic-district code, anyway, a sticker amidst the clematis vines.

"Would you open on Sunday for his schedule?" the sous-chef asked.

"It's not like he won't win if he doesn't have dinner here on Sunday," the chef said.

"The Secret Service has to come first," the hostess-owner said. "They searched the planters with flashlights. They guarded the bathroom and searched it every time anyone went in and out."

"We're surrounded by weapons here," the sous-chef said. "Knives of all kinds."

"They came in earlier to prepare," the hostess-owner said. "They were here forever. They said, 'We need a "safe room" if there's an attack.' I freaked when they said that. They were like, 'We'll keep the military dogs there.' I'm like, 'Oh, attack, right.'"

"We better do the order," the sous-chef said. "My wife is waiting for me. My kid is asleep."

"This is why I'll never have children," the chef said. "I'm too devoted to my work."

The chef had told us how hard he worked when he changed the menu. He had to shower, shave, and put on clean clothes before he began the arduous task. He had to be rested.

"I wear a clean white bathrobe and nightgown when I start sorting photos at night," I said.

"I put on a clean white bathrobe and nightgown, too," he said. Then he laughed a mad laugh. "The menu is an artistic creation." He looked serious again.

"Our waiter-actor wants to have kids," the sous-chef said.

"How?" the waitress asked.

"He's the only one who doesn't think he's gay," the sous-chef said.

"That's because of the way he looks and the way he understands things," I said.

"He doesn't say how. But he has the names all picked out—Bambi and Roland. He loves children."

"Let's order," the chef said.

"Is it the same menu?" someone asked.

"Why does everyone ask that?" the chef said. "A friend came

by and said, 'Is this going to be the menu for the whole season?'
I said, 'Don't come here anymore. You're not my friend.'"

Restaurant activities were emerging from the kitchen doorway. Big rubber pails of garbage and ice were shoved around
here and there. To watch this was as privileged a position as
being allowed to stand in the dish room, the way John Kerry
did.

"We don't let everyone see this," the chef said. "You're one
of the lucky ones."

The sous-chef started to read from a yellow lined pad: "OR-
CHIDS, SALMON, PEACHES, FIGS—AVOCADO, MIXED BLOSSOMS, POME-
GRANATE, PEPPERCORNS."

Right in the midst of the smoking, the wine, the talk of the
chin, the melted ice, and the garbage came this poem.

"Is that the real list?" I asked. I felt a small mania coming on.
I thought these items would make a good photo.

"Everyone loves to hear our list," the chef said with a dulled-
down pride.

"It's the way I do it, in iambic pentameter," the sous-chef
said. "It's from reading to my son—Dr. Seuss and all that gives
me the rhythm." He had mentioned that he'd majored in literature in college.

People on the staff finished their chores and left while the
chef was still writing his orders and talking about the world situation.

"I have so much more to do," he said. "Then, the last thing,
right before I leave, I close the windows and turn off the lights.

I walk home and I look at the sky, I go in the door, I greet my dog, we go out walking around the town."

It sounded sad to me.

After I left I couldn't get the words out of my head: "OR-CHIDS, SALMON, PEACHES, FIGS——AVOCADO, MIXED BLOSSOMS, POME-GRANATE, PEPPERCORNS." As I walked down the crooked brick sidewalk in the dark, I kept thinking about the words and how they sounded.

EVEN WEEKS later, in September, it was still best to avoid the town during the day.

When I passed by the diner on my bike at five o'clock, I saw that the hostess-owner was outside sweeping. She was wearing a long pink dress and low, pointy-heeled sandals. She had a Cin-derella look in the way she swept.

I stepped into the doorway and saw the chef walking to the stove. He was carrying a giant soup ladle slung over his shoul-der. The sous-chef was walking behind him. Both wore white T-shirts and looked as if they worked in a prison. They had the facial expressions that went with prison life.

The chef went over to a gigantic vat on the stove and started stirring with the ladle.

"What's in the pot?" I asked as I opened the screen door.

"Curry sauce," he said, and kept stirring.

That night, I walked back into town. I was around the corner from the restaurant, and from that distance I could hear loud noise coming from the alley. It was the kind of screaming-laughing and shouting generated by alcohol. Why wasn't alcohol classified along with the other addictive, dangerous drugs? As I passed the alley, I could smell cigar smoke, a sign of Republicans.

I was on my way to the late-night bookstore. For a year I'd been trying to buy that book of essays by Paul Krugman, but the big red-and-white cover was too hard to look at. The paperback might be smaller and less red.

When I walked back from the bookstore, the noise from the restaurant alley was still going on. A waitress came out through the screen door. "There's a party of thirteen asses on the patio," she said.

"I could hear the screaming from Main Street," I said.

"Drinking is big with Republicans," she said. "But drunk driving should be a disqualification for the office of president."

"Plus a really low IQ," I said.

She went back inside to wait on the loud group.

I COMPARED the demeanor of the thirteen asses to what I imagined to be that of the Democratic candidate's dinner on the patio back in July. The very first time I'd seen him was on Main Street, where he was leaving the beverage store with a bottle of wine in hand. As he waved the bottle in the direction of the clerk, he had that put-it-on-the-account gesture people from his background use. He had it down pat.

That was August 17, 1997, the night of President Clinton's televised apology. I assumed that the wine-charging senator was going home to watch the apology, and that he and his family needed the anesthesia.

As he walked down Main Street around to Center Street, he was stopped by constituents every few minutes, and he stood and talked to them in that beaten-down, disappointed-with-others posture he has. I wanted to join the group and ask, "Can't something be done to put an end to this immediately?" It was his job to stand on the brick sidewalk and answer questions. He wasn't a rock star. I watched from across the street and saw him walk off in the opposite direction. He walked fast, even though it was a hot, humid evening.

I WAS standing and listening to the noisy Republicans. The hostess-owner came out. Her long flared skirt flipped around her like a dancer's skirt in a musical from the nineteen-fifties. If only John Raitt would come out and start singing "Oklahoma," I thought.

Instead, the thirteen asses began emerging from the alley. The women in the group tried to stagger toward the hostess and say, "Fabulous"—the real F-word, in my opinion. They all had names like Arlene and Sheila. They couldn't help it: those were their names. But what about the behavior?

I'd heard a conversation at the other end of the island, and the diners weren't even drunk.

Since it was a Sunday night, we had to go out there to a tiny café. It was the only other place with open windows. I spotted a Republican foursome sitting across from us. They were an upper-middle-aged foursome, but seemed to be having a good time in spite of their stage in life. One of the women was dressed all in pink—pink sweater, pink slacks, pink pearls, and a pink silk scarf. She wore a number of gold bracelets and a big diamond ring. The ring sparkled across their table toward the other tables. Her blond hair was blown into a straight, plain style that I could tell she'd worn since high school. I had just picked up my salad fork when I heard her say the word "medals."

"He 'sort of' risked his life, but then he used it for political purposes" was what she said next.

The others agreed with her. They said it over in different ways but none could outdo the words "sort of."

"My father has two Purple Hearts, from serving during World War II," she said. "And I'm proud of his service, but he always told us the medals weren't for anything, really. That was his view of it."

"Where are the medals?" her husband asked.

"In the drawer in the main upstairs hall," she said, naming a piece of furniture I'd never heard of. Not a credenza, whatever that is—I made a note to look it up in a Martha Stewart book—but a higher-class furniture name than that. She'd gotten all that into the sentence: her father in the war, the being proud of that, the winning of the medals, the agreement that the medals were for nothing.

I checked out her husband, the one who wanted to know where the medals were kept. He was smiling as if he approved of his wife's summation. I'd put my fork down and given up any notion of placing even a microgreen on it. I didn't want to be holding a weaponlike instrument, even though I had no wish to attack the couple with it. Maybe it was an unconscious wish.

It was at that moment that I noticed the husband's slacks. They weren't Nantucket red—the light, faded, strange red— they were really red, dark red. And with these dark-red pants, he wore an expensive-looking white sweater over a white shirt.

After putting the medal subject to rest, the two couples looked at each other with silent contentment. The other husband was all in white. He was a big, Liberace kind of guy; a tall, overweight guy with white hair, white pants, white sweater, gold watchband. He was a Liberace–George Hamilton– Fernando Lamas kind of guy, and he'd stretched his long, soft-looking white legs out to better enjoy the relaxing conversation, the dinner, and the summer evening.

Behind this foursome was a large window. It was hooked open, with two window boxes full of flowers almost touching the backs of their chairs. The words "sort of" were still hanging over their table as I watched them contemplate other current events. I wished I could fork up those words and fling them out the window into the night.

The older woman said she "liked to think" they had some

very good senators in their southern state. She named one senator I'd seen wearing a bad toupée. Then the two couples returned to sharing their dessert, lemon custard in pie crust.

I WAS planning to leave Nantucket sometime. But when? Every time I made a plan, the ferry was canceled due to a windstorm.

Unlike people who have lives with planned dates, I tried to live according to the weather, like a sailor or a farmer. Because the Weather Channel was my favorite, travel plans were made easier. One year, I was pressured to stay until November by my work project and also things people said about the weather. "You can't leave now," they all said.

The Jamaican cleaning helper would stand on the porch and speak for herself: "I love Nantucket, I just love it. It's so beautiful. It's so peaceful. Even just over there." She was looking over at a corner where there was a tree, a blue-green evergreen shrub, and a flowering shrub—all this green in the afternoon light.

"I just love it here," she'd say over and over.

I WAS lucky or unlucky enough to get a ferry reservation between the windstorms. When I told the pharmacist that I was leaving soon, he said, "You can't leave! It's just getting good. And your homeopathic allergy eyedrops won't be in yet."

I was involved in photographing some grass and berries in some moors—each day they looked different, and my plan was to photograph every plant growing on Nantucket.

"You have to go home to vote," people said when the subject came up. Except for the actor-waiter. When I mentioned voting as a reason for leaving, he said, "Is one better than the other? Does it matter?"

"One is worse than the other," I said.

We'd been on such friendly terms, and now this.

"I haven't really had time to follow," he said.

The next day I left for my home state in order to vote.

I WAS lying in bed. There was no reason to get up. It was morning, but there was a feeling of darkness outside, inside, and crushing down from above. Maybe the darkness was due, in part, to the awnings, which should have been removed for November and the time change. Or maybe it was because we had planted out the neighbor's house and the greenhouse sun to the degree that we had blocked out the light.

A nuclear bomb hadn't exploded, as far as I knew, but the darkness was of the kind I'd seen in films about nuclear bombs—or nucular, as the Alfred E. Neuman president liked to say. Will this never be corrected or brought to the attention of the world? Are the other heads of nations just being polite?

I knew that the Polish bulb-planting man was scheduled to come help plant hundreds of bulbs I'd over-ordered in a manic spree. But I'd have to get up to do that. I took the phone from under a pillow and found his cell number in the call log. I asked him about coming on Thursday instead. "It's really windy," I said.

"I'd better come Thursday," he said. "Because you sound sick. So I shouldn't come today."

"I'm sick about the election," I said. "I don't have a cold. I was crying."

"Me too!" he said. "I'm sick, too. Everybody is!"

"But are you planting bulbs?" I asked.

"Sure I'm planting. I'm raking leaves. Branches are falling all over from the wind. You can't imagine what we have here, how we are working in the wind."

The man had a Polish accent and a Polish rhythm of speaking English words.

"I have extra time today," he said. "Nobody wants to plant bulbs. They don't care. They are all in their homes crying."

"Okay," I said. "Come today."

I was looking at the closed window blind from my position in bed. Although darkness was everywhere, in my room and in the outside world, the sun was out and the wind was blowing the branches and the leaves that were still on the branches. The leaves were making a swirling light between the whitewashed wood slats of the blinds. I'd been lying in bed watching this sight for a while before I called the bulb planter.

Earlier that morning, I had started to prepare for the day and was almost dressed and ready to go outside in a tan corduroy skirt and a white flannel shirt—my thought was that light colors are cheerful—when I'd had the idea, not that it can be called an idea, to go back to bed. Not wanting to mix outside clothing with clean white sheets and blankets, I had taken off my clothes and put on a white bathrobe to get back into bed. Into the bed, into the sheets, to be one with the bed and the night, the not knowing about this day.

From my position in bed, I could see that the course of the natural day—of sunlight, of outside, of wind and leaves and trees—the day was continuing on in spite of what had happened. Worse things in history have happened on beautiful days—an illustration of Dr. Andrew Weil's advice not to read or listen to the news. But still I didn't have the strength to fight back, and I let the weight of the world press down, the way the iron grilling weight pressed down whatever the chef was cooking the life out of on the grill.

I knew only a fragment of the news from having watched *The Daily Show,* where a few news facts could be discerned from the jokes. This was the main flaw in the show.

One or two election facts had crept in. I'd spent the rest of the night watching the Weather Channel without the newly defunct 2:00 a.m. rerun of Martha Stewart's program—so beautiful and peaceful to see, with the exception of the cooking segment, where no consciousness had been raised with Martha for animal rights. I'd heard her say the words "baby lamb chops." Is she bad, is she good, what is she really?

My first call after going back to bed was to the elderly nursery owner, to ask a question about bulb planting. The owner said she had forced herself to get up after lying in bed until ten. "I couldn't go to church this morning," she said. "And I go every day. This is the first time ever that's happened."

She said that no one had gone to the service. When people were called to see where they were, they said they couldn't get out of bed. What would the religious right say to that, I was wondering, but didn't have the energy to think it through. They have an answer for everything. They'd make one up for that, too.

I got up. I put on my clothes. Outside on the grass, in the sunlight with the bulb man and his rosy-cheeked Polish helper, it was still impossible to escape the feeling of doom. It surrounded us and followed us in the open air. Trying to figure out where to plant which bulbs distracted us for only a minute or two.

The Polish bulb man was in a fury about the election. I had already diagnosed high blood pressure from the sight of his chubby red face, and I was worried that he might have a stroke, the way the great *New York Review of Books* journalist Lars-Erik Nelson had a fatal stroke while watching the Supreme Court decision on the news, in the aftermath of the last fraudulent election, four years earlier. I also had in mind the lesser fear that the bulbs wouldn't get planted.

In the spring, the bulb man had told me that he couldn't plant in wet weather because he had gout. The name of the disease had a medieval ring to it. But could he plant in political anger was the question now.

Before he'd left in the spring, I gave him a copy of *Eating Well for Optimum Health,* but I could tell that he was a sausage lover and wouldn't give them up for his medical condition.

In our mutually dazed state, we walked around looking for the right place for this bag of bulbs and that. Every now and then, the other subject would come up.

"I can't believe this happened!" he said. His outburst went on long enough to use the word "ass" for the Republican so-called president.

"There must be some hope," I said. "It's not final yet."

"Yes, yes, it is over! I heard at one o'clock!"

People are always telling you news you don't need to know. On the other hand, after hearing a bulletin like that, there would be no reason to worry about what blooms when.

"Can you vote?" I asked the man.

"Not yet," he said. "I'm getting my citizenship soon. Next time I will vote. Damn! Four more years of this!"

"More than four," I said as I looked down at the brown paper bags of bluebells. I had bought too many for our small space, but at the same time, I hadn't bought enough. There can never be enough.

"It will take years to undo the damage," I said. "Maybe never. They can end the world tomorrow."

"What a bunch of asses!" he said as he picked up his shovel. "You need more pink mix for the daffodils."

"I'll see if they're still shipping," I said. Ten years ago, bulb companies wouldn't ship after November first, but in the new greenhouse climate, they shipped until December.

I had heard a Republican apologist for global warming counter evidence of the problem with this: "People like warm weather. That's the reason they go south. It won't be a problem. It will be an asset." The bulb-shipping schedule must have been an example of that.

AFTER THE bulb man left, I had enough time to walk three miles on the conservation land. In order not to miss the light while hiking and trying to photograph the last light of the dark day, I took the bulb catalogue along with me. Cell phones were forbidden on the conservation land, but no one else was there. I called the bulb company and looked at the pages of daffodils as I walked and ordered into the earpiece. I hoped I wouldn't be caught calling out names of pink daffodils into the tiny microphone.

As I walked, I had to name the daffodils and these names were nothing I wanted to say: Felicity, Faithful, High Society, Kissproof, and Eastern Dawn. Just as bad were people's names—Professor Einstein was one of them. One has to wonder who named tulips and iris and daffodils, just as one wonders who names pharmaceutical drugs. Poetic assistance could be used in both industries.

Most of the pink mix was sold out, and I was down to ordering individual names, even the Tommy's White. The name Tom was associated with those two Toms in government offices—the one in the clownlike, color-filled, so-called Security

Department; the other, a secretary of something else. The name had fallen into disfavor in whichever part of the brain names are stored and connected to faces and actions.

As I walked fast over hill and valley, over the bridge, across the pond, and up to the ocean, I realized that I had ordered enough. I was going to end the call without making a political statement to the operator. From my selection of colors and petal shapes, my political position could be known.

T HE WEEK ended. I never watched the news. The *New York Times* stayed in the driveway all day. At night I threw it into the recycling bin.

The bulbs arrived; the rain stopped; the man came back to finish planting. We didn't mention the election. We looked down at the bags of bulbs we still had to plant.

"What is Feerflee?" he asked.

I read the label: "Firefly." I couldn't remember the color of the crocus.

"We'll do the crocuses next week," the man said. "It's start-ing to rain."

The Firefly must have been lavender, along with all of the other ones, an inspiration from the planting outside one of Martha Stewart's houses, where I'd seen thousands of lavender crocuses in bloom.

★   ★   ★

I WAS thinking about the world. This is a mistake and can lead to insanity.

This is where the Travel and Weather Channel comes in. They show the world, then the planet, the earth spinning in the universe. As it spins—all green earth and blue water, without people or cars—it becomes larger until it's a close-up of just where you live, turning into the United States of America, then your state, then your town, enlarged, with details of the local weather right there. Your local weather is the only thing, described every two minutes for twenty-four hours. Those who can't meditate can watch this.

THE NEXT week, some books arrived from the bookstore. One was the paperback edition of the book by Paul Krugman about the great unraveling. The bookstore owner had included a smaller brown paper bag with miniature botanical prints from a medicinal plant series—valerian, goldenseal, echinacea among them—nothing to cure the condition that afflicted the world. Then I saw that on the bag the bookstore owner had written a note: A LITTLE PRESENT ON THIS DARK NOVEMBER DAY.

I looked at the sad little bag with the handwritten sentence and I decided to save it. I'd save it and frame it along with the tiny prints, and also another saved note written on a paper napkin. It was the kind of napkin that comes prefolded into a rectangle and embossed with a shell pattern. The author was the Jamaican cleaning helper. She'd written:

DEAR ———,

Good evening, I came and straighten

up kitchen Did the

White Table and start

To Iron, but my head

was hurting me. So

I am gone to the

Pharmacy.

I call you later.

———

I'd frame these things and hang them up next to a cheap paper napkin I'd found, already framed, at an antiques store in 1978. The napkin was opened up into a flat square, and all around the border someone had carefully painted a circle of little American flags.

I had hoped to send the flag napkin to John Kerry as an Inauguration Day present and to commemorate his dining at the diner-restaurant—though they used cloth napkins there—and also to commend his patriotism. The cheapness of the background of the napkin would symbolize the tawdriness of our present civilization, and at the same time the endless dining out in our country, while there is no dining at all in some other countries. If John Kerry liked the primitive wooden door in the restaurant alley, he might like the flag napkin. Or he might not. What difference would it make? There was nothing else I could do.

THANK YOU FOR THE MITTENS

I HAD A FRIEND in the town where we lived. I was driving down a lane toward her house, but I wasn't planning to see her. I was planning to leave a small shopping bag with a present on her porch door.

It was almost dusk. The dark, peaceful winter nights were my favorite times—the tall, three-hundred-year-old trees with branches making archways over the empty lanes and roads.

The friend was someone I wanted to thank for her present to me, mittens she'd knitted in a peach color she knew to be my favorite. One thing she'd forgotten was that I can't wear wool or mohair, or even touch it.

When I saw the beautiful, thick, fuzzy things, I planned to order some heavy silk mitten liners from the winter silk catalogue. But I knew it would be tricky even to touch the mittens in order to put them on.

In childhood, my mother argued with me, insisting that various winter garments were not scratching my skin. She also insisted I try on long woolen underwear to wear for ice-skating the way everyone else in the family did. This refusal to wear wool set me apart from the rest of the family at an early age. When my mother saw the rashes on the insides of my arms, she conceded that an allergy to wool was possible, and the rash was treated with Baby Magic, a pink, perfumed lotion used for such purposes at the time. We didn't know the ingredients.

Even worse, time after time, for a minor ailment, the family doctor convinced her to give me a liquid sulfa drug, also pink. They didn't believe that the resulting itching throat was a sign of a serious allergy to sulfa. When the allergic reaction—the swelling of the throat and tongue—nearly asphyxiated me, the doctor and my mother both began to believe that sulfa caused allergies. The treatment for this was standing around the bed and watching. I don't recall Benadryl being administered in any form. A call for an ambulance wasn't considered.

The peach mittens made me think of mittens my mother had knitted for me when I was nine or ten. She was often talking about increasing or decreasing stitches—advanced steps in the knitting world. The knitting went on while she watched Groucho Marx on *You Bet Your Life*, which she thought was one of the only good things on TV. *What's My Line?* was the other. She was at the same stage of life as my friend, the stage that I'd described to the friend as "women flailing about, trying to find meaning in their lives." My friend said, "I know the feeling."

My mother had knitted navy-blue-and-white-striped mittens and a matching hat with earflaps and a long tassel on top of the hat. For some reason, maybe because she was an artiste man-quée, she added a small silver bell to the end of the tassel. My friends ridiculed the bell; maybe the entire hat, too. But I knew it was a work of art even though it scratched my ears and neck. A red rash appeared under my chin.

This era coincided with the beginning of rock and roll and Elvis Presley. Like former President Clinton, I'm glad I was alive during that time. I'd heard him say this in a talk he gave about his book. I recall that part as the most interesting thing he said about his life.

In this era, if any head covering was worn, it was supposed to be a scarf. There's a well-known photograph of Priscilla Pres-ley wearing a scarf this way at age twelve or thirteen. No hat at all was the favorite style, even on the coldest days. Also desir-able were white angora headbands—about four inches wide—that covered the ears and tied under the chin. There were a few white sequins scattered through the angora. When I pointed out these headbands to my mother she knitted one for me, but in a superior and fluffier angora than the kind used in the machine-made version. She sewed many more sequins onto the beautiful object. Both of these deviations from the norm were criticized by my classmates. The headgear, too fluffy; the se-quins, too many. Everyone was supposed to wear the same exact thing as everyone else.

★ ★ ★

W HEN I saw the peach mittens I could see how they'd been knitted with separate needles and then knitted to connect the two sides to a point, unlike those done by my mother, who rounded out the tips. My friend had not mastered the technique of decreasing.

I remembered being told by a clever twelve-year-old boy that a middle-aged professor— a colleague of the boy's father—had had a mental breakdown that resulted in his crying while talking about mittens his mother had knit for him when he was a child. I no longer found the memory of the boy's telling of the story amusing, the way I had just a few years before.

My friend's favorite things to bake were Christmas cookies. She began talking about them in early November. She talked fast—about this kind and that kind. I'd seen some like these before, in bakeries. My friend's more unusual cookies were thin and delicate—the Christmas tree, the Santa's boot, the star, the gingerbread man—all sprinkled with sugar crystals that looked like tiny glass snowflakes.

One year, when the ponds froze solid for two weeks, all she did was bake, and ice-skate three times a day. I asked whether she put the cookies in tins and gave them away as presents. She said no, they were all for her and her family— mostly for her.

I wanted to see all those cookies, not to have any for myself. She once led me to a secret pantry and opened tin after tin filled with cookies. Finally she took out a tiny boot and said, "Do you want one?"

I said, "It's beautiful, should we share it?"

She said okay, and we did.

I HAD given her a jar of lavender-scented oil-and-salt scrub that I knew she'd like to use on her skin in her outdoor shower. She'd told me how she made her own scrub—she made her own everything, like a pioneer woman.

I thought this lavender salt scrub would be a special treat. But when she said, "What is it?," and I had to explain, I got the idea that it wasn't such a good present. "April fifteenth," she said. "I'll open it then." That was when she started the outdoor salt-scrubbing. She did have lustrous, youthful skin for a woman our age, over forty-nine. Her skin is thicker than mine—not one broken capillary or visible vein. Her legs look twenty-five years old. If I scrub too hard, I may scrub away my skin completely. Thin white skin doesn't last as long as thick, tan skin, I've found out in this decade of finding out things about skin and bones.

After I took off my jacket, my friend admired my undershirt—the cotton lace part that was showing under a bigger, man's shirt. I told her my everyday undershirts were still wet from the laundry, and I'd had to wear this better one. "It's not my best, I have one I save for special occasions."

Although she has no interest in clothes, she admired the undershirt with intensity and even asked where I'd gotten it. I told her where, I told her it had an Italian label, I'd gotten it on sale, and it was five years old. I made an instant plan to buy her one. I knew they'd be on sale again at a certain store in the town. One afternoon, through the window, I'd seen young women crowding around a table in a vulturelike way, as if the sale had started.

On this visit, when I was trying to leave my friend's present on the porch, she heard my footsteps on the brick path. She came to the door to invite me in to see the Christmas tree and the new dog.

A year before, I'd left a white amaryllis out on the porch. She and her husband were surprised when they came home from an Al-Anon meeting for their teenage son. They both thanked me in a way that seemed to mean they'd never received an amaryllis before.

I'd spent time seeking out a pot with green moss growing on it, and asked the nursery man to put some feather moss on the soil around the stem. Then he wrapped the whole thing in cellophane and tied it with raffia. He had this down pat and helped me do some plant presents every year.

I felt I had to send these to anyone who had helped me in any way in our new cruel and tough society. Doctors, just for giving an appointment or calling back; friends who have listened to dark thoughts—these are on the ever-growing list.

Standing in the potting room and finding the right pot and the moss was time-consuming, but worth the result. The nursery man had a lot of energy to talk and explain horticultural facts, and he ran back and forth getting just the right plant and right pot, although I bought only a few and he had clients in the town who bought a hundred.

When I thought about it later, I realized that I'd never received an amaryllis, or any plant, as a present. I guessed I'd be appreciative, too, especially if I had a son whose problems were causing me to go to Al-Anon meetings in a small town, and I came home to find a flowering plant. But I didn't have that son, and was at the stage of life where friends would say, "You're lucky." People have these problems with sons now.

On this evening, when my friend insisted that I come in to see the tree and the dog, I was tempted. I'd been planning to go for a walk in the last light of the damp and drizzly New Year's Eve. Walking and exercise were the priorities. I said this each day to myself and my friend. She was the physically fittest person I knew. She swam, hiked, NordicTracked—she'd made it into a verb—raked leaves, and shoveled snow. It was a long list of physical activities, but still she talked me out of the walk. "You can't walk in this weather," she'd said, but she was wrong. It would be bracing, refreshing, and aerobic. The drawback was the aloneness.

S HE GOT me to come in and sit down in the library room filled with old books. Sitting isn't aerobic.

"Come say hello," she called to the son who was in the

kitchen. Why would an eighteen-year-old boy want to say hello to me, I wondered as he came in and said it while making the extra effort to smile.

"We don't have many visitors," my friend said. "It's nice to have someone come over."

I thought she did have lots of visitors—when I'd phoned her on one occasion she'd said, "We're in the middle of a knitting, crocheting, and quilting bee. Would you like to come over?" I said, "No, thanks," as fast as I could, too fast perhaps, but I really didn't want to sit around with women doing this stuff. Maybe if they'd had one gay guy there, too, that would have been fun.

"Don't you want to watch the BBC news?" I asked.

"It's almost over," she said.

"You like the PBS *NewsHour*."

"My son doesn't like it," she said.

I didn't ask why. I assumed he didn't like the news, not the program. I agreed with this view.

I will always have a fond spot in my former heart for Jim Lehrer because of his tomato show in the seventies or eighties. The topic was why tomatoes don't taste like tomatoes anymore. The guest was an elderly man from a tomato-growers' association. He said the tomato problem was the fault of "the housewife." "The housewife" buys the tomatoes when they're not ripe—it was okay with him that they were shipped hard and green. "The housewife" puts them in the refrigerator, where they'll never ripen and turn red. "The housewife" places them stem-side-up on the windowsill. The stem side is tougher and should go down; the other, thinner-skinned side must go up. Everything was the fault of "the housewife."

I watched Jim Lehrer control his amusement, and his possibly learned feminism, while this went on. Then he said—paraphrased here—"In our house, I'm the one who buys the tomatoes, and I don't do any of those things. I do what you recommend and the tomatoes are still mealy and don't taste the way tomatoes should taste."

When the boy left the room, we checked out the *NewsHour* for a moment. The so-called president was on, telling one of his many lies in his most incompetent manner. "Liar!" my friend and I both shouted at the same time to the screen. We were like Elvis Presley shooting a gun at the TV when Robert Goulet was singing. It just happened. That's friendship. Then we turned the TV off. We can't let rage cancel out our other healthy habits.

Then she went into the kitchen to see about something on the stove. Some housework was always going on in that kitchen. When she was in there I heard her say, "Oh, no, the dog has eaten the whole chocolate cake!"

She came back and began a frantic cross-examination-style questioning of her son. Where was he when the incident occurred? Why wasn't the dog gated into the library? How did he get out?

"That's why we need two gates," she confided in me.

"I don't know how it happened," her son said. "I was sleeping the whole time."

I'd forgotten about that—the recovery from the substance, this time a mind-expanding-substance experiment that went awry. Certainly it did the trick in the mind-expansion department—on a recent walk on the conservation land with us, he'd said, "This looks like Mars." He was right. It did, in a way: all sand and hills and barren sand paths in between, with dried-out sand plants and foliage.

Before his mind had been expanded, he was a regular teenager, but a sexist variety with unrealistic plans for his future life—being taken care of by women in some place like Costa Rica. After the breakdown due to the substance, and then the medication to cure that, he was a more pleasant eighteen-year-old boy. He seemed to have grown a few inches in addition to the mind growth, looking about six foot six. He'd lost a bit of weight, creating the messed-up-model look in one of those designed-to-be-messy ads for casual clothes and wild living.

"Now I have to call the vet—dogs can die from eating chocolate," my friend said. She went to the phone. Because it was almost New Year's Eve, she had to leave a message on the vet's machine. She sat down next to me on the couch. The dog was napping peacefully—or maybe not.

"He looks okay," she said.

"No, he doesn't," the son said. "He looks sick."

"Isn't this how dogs always act?" I asked. He was one of the big Labs who all act alike.

"I hope he doesn't die," my friend said. "I was getting to like him." She looked down at the sleeping dog. "Oh, well."

"How could you eat a whole chocolate cake?" the son asked the dog as he patted the animal's head.

"Wasn't it good?" I asked the dog.

The son laughed as if that were funnier than it was.

"I didn't know dogs died from chocolate-eating," I said.

My friend leaned back on the sofa cushion and directed an exhausted glance toward the animal. She was wearing a fuzzy pink sweater, and pink makes me feel calm, so I kept looking at it. I knew why pink was the color used for padded cells in institutions.

The small Christmas tree was decorated with cards with photos of people's children. I never want to look at that kind of thing. I like to look at ornaments.

If people send me a Christmas card with a family photo I tear it up right away and throw it into the recycling bin. I couldn't look at the tree. Through the window, I could see a grey-lavender dusk coming on, and I wished that I could be out in this dusk. The tall boy was sitting on a chair acting normal.

"Nice sweater," I said to my friend. "I love that color."

"Old ladies look good in pink," she said. She smiled—it was the "old" thing again. It's a joke we had. One of those true jokes. It's coming fast to everyone in our generation.

My friend had blue eyes and pure white straight hair down to her shoulders. It was one of those fifty-year-old-model looks, the kind where white hair starts early, in the thirties or twenties. I remembered my mother telling me that if only her hair would turn white she wouldn't have to color it. "White is good, grey is bad," she'd say. Early on in childhood, I used to tell her to dye her hair pitch-black like Elizabeth Taylor's. This truth is what my mother said: "Black is harsh and aging. She's young enough to get away with it." Next Elvis Presley and Roy Orbison got away with it. Craig Ferguson didn't. Paul McCartney has problems with dark brown.

These are the kinds of truths my mother knew, but busy with important thoughts, she had little time to spare for explaining any more about hair coloring.

"We're not old yet," I said to my friend. "You just look good in pink."

The phone rang and she jumped up. It was an old wall phone. She quickly began telling the story of the cake, standing and reciting the exact ingredients. "Four squares of baking chocolate, four eggs, one cup of sugar, one cup of flour—and the dog weighs sixty-seven pounds." She has a stern, military style when she gets into her efficient mode. Then she listened for a second or two and said, "Oh, the icing! I forgot the icing." She began to recite the ingredients for that: "Two more squares of Baker's chocolate." Soon she hung up.

"He's not going to die, I don't think," she said. "It was the vet's assistant. It goes by the weight of the dog."

"Look on Ask Dr. Weil," I said. "He has two dogs."

"What kind?" the son asked.

"Rhodesian ridgebacks," I said.

"All the cool people have those," he said.

"But why?" I asked.

"They just do. Don't know why."

"I don't like them," my friend said.

"Well, look it up. He knows all about chocolate and the drug that's in it. Theobromine. It's an upper and a downer at the same time," I said. "Or something like that."

That horrible thing, the computer, was in the room with us. It was the bad kind—big, and wired into the wall with a cable. My friend got up and did something to turn it on. Then she said to her son, "You do it. I have to wait for the vet to call."

"Okay," he said and went to sit in a chair in front of the thing. He was so tall that he had to put his feet up on top of the radiator cover under the window. It was a beautiful old radiator cover, metal caning with a small flower pattern appliquéd in the middle of the border. I noticed that the boy was barefoot and was wearing the same grey sweatshirt and pants he was wearing on my last visit.

"'Is chocolate deadly for dogs?'" he read aloud, finding the right question and answer immediately. "'The size and breed of the dog and the amount consumed determine' et cetera . . . 'Chocolate contains theobromine, a drug in the same family as caffeine. One ounce per nine pounds of body weight for Baker's Chocolate.' That would be toxic. 'Symptoms include hyperactivity.'" He stopped and looked at the sleeping dog and he started to laugh.

"There, same as the vet said," he told us.

"That's a relief," my friend said. "Can you go and scold him for what he did?" she asked her son.

"I'm not good at scolding," he said.

"I've never gotten over a similar situation from childhood where I was told to scold our family cat," I said. "PETA should come and get me."

"But that's how you train them," my friend said.

"They shouldn't be trained by humans," I said. "They're meant to live outside with their own kind. Why should they have to follow the rules of humans in houses?"

"That's true. They're meant to live in packs with each other," she said.

"See? How would you like to be forced to live outside with them and their rules?" I said.

"True, true," she said. The phone rang and she jumped up. It was her husband. He was on the way home.

"These scenes are always happening with dogs," I said.

I was beginning to feel sick about the whole situation. "Why don't you open your present?" I said.

"That's a good idea. You didn't have to bring another present."

"I wanted to. You'll see why."

"Is it dog- or cake-related?"

"No, it's for your own personal self," I said.

She took the box and began to untie the ribbon. It was all white—the box, the tissue paper, the Italian undershirt, the white cotton lace straps and lace that went around the front and back. Its all-white purity didn't fit into the scene, but it would be a distraction for us. She picked it up by the straps and said, "Oh, beautiful. Thank you."

"It's not the same one you admired. It's like my first best one, the one I save for the most special occasions, which don't exist anymore."

"Oh, I love it," she said as she looked at the undershirt.

"You know, it looks small," I said. "I should have gotten medium. Suddenly it looks tiny. And I almost got extra small."

"Small is the right size," she said, standing and holding it up against the pink sweater. I'd been picturing her perfect thin legs and bottom half when I chose the size. I had recently noticed in profile that this half of her looked about three inches wide from this angle. "I didn't know you had . . ."

"Breasts?" she said.

"No, shoulder and arm muscles of that size. Try it on. I can call and ask for a medium. They're open until six."

She went into the kitchen. "Don't come in," she said to her son, who was still reading Dr. Weil's advice. "I'm taking my shirt off."

Her son gave her a look with a benevolent smile. "She's crazy and I'll go along with it" was the smile. He didn't say anything. People had ways to deal with the behavior of others. I was always trying to learn these ways instead of arguing, my first choice.

My friend's daughter had a different method. I noticed it when my friend was describing how she cooked a five-gallon pot of rice and other gallon pots of three kinds of beans, and then divided them into containers that she froze for quick dinners. This description had been going on in her speedy style, as she tried to get in all the details of the efficiency behind the method.

That time we were in the living room for an occasion like Christmas or Thanksgiving, the kind where a few friends are invited to keep the family from getting into their usual conversations and arguments.

The daughter looked at me—I guessed because I was smiling—and she mouthed the words "She's crazy!" She also used that crazy-meaning hand gesture, index finger going in a circle near the temple.

But your mother is my friend, I was thinking. I thought she and I were on the same team. We were, sort of, grown women. But things had changed since our youth. Ages were all mixed up together now.

The reason I was smiling was because I, too, liked to freeze beans in containers, but didn't have the efficiency or freezer space to do it in quantities of this kind. It was the sped-up, frantic recitation that made me smile. I didn't have four children, a dog, a full-time job, and a husband who expected to be served regular daily meals. I'd trained my husband to expect no more cooking when my work took over.

I had reminded my friend many times that we were from the feminist era. For a few years I'd tried saying, "But you went to

Radcliffe," and she'd say, "But I dropped out and got married."
Then I'd say, "But some of it had to sink in."

"Apparently not," she'd say in her brusque style.

Then I switched to "Housework is the enemy of the artist."
Sometimes I couldn't be sure who said it and attributed the
quote to Louise Nevelson.

"I'm not an artist," she'd say. "I'm a professor."

"You can't be in the kitchen all the time," I'd say.

"I'm not," she'd say. "Sometimes I'm hanging laundry out on
the line."

M Y FRIEND came back out of the kitchen in the lace-trimmed
undershirt. "It's fine," she said. "Don't you think?"

"Does it feel tight?" I asked.

"No, it feels good," she said. "Don't look," she said to her
son, who was slowly trying to get up for some other reason.

"It's okay for him to see it," I said to her. "It looks like a top
people wear outside—more modest actually."

"It looks like a top," her son agreed, with nonchalant knowledge of the lewd fashions that girls of his generation wore and
which he took in stride.

"Women wear underclothes outside now," I said.

"How can you tell?" she said. "If it's all the same."

"This is better," I said. "The Italians have the best everything—vegetables, fabric, designs, paintings, chapels."

"The Renaissance," she said.

The phone rang. It was the vet. Back into her sweater, she went over the conclusion with him. I heard her say, "Peroxide?" She listened and thanked him and hung up.

"I hope you won't give him peroxide," I said.

"It's not necessary, fortunately."

We were back looking at the dog again. The undershirt was lying on the box.

"Let's put it away," I said. "It should be separated from this conversation."

She put it into the box.

"He must be gated at all times," my friend said. "He can't go into the kitchen."

"Get another gate," the son said.

"I'm too tired to go buy another gate at this late hour," my friend said.

"I'm going to get some dinner to eat," the son said.

"Okay." Then she called after him, "Leave a lot for Dad."

I'd never heard of such a thing—telling a growing teenager to leave a lot of food for Dad. Isn't there always food and food and food for children and their fathers, too?

A Welshman I used to know had told me that during the rationing of World War II, the one egg would be given to the youngest child, and everyone in the family would watch while the child smashed the egg all over his face and high-chair tray instead of eating it. I recently saw the Welshman on C-SPAN— he'd become a member of Parliament.

"Okay," the boy called back from the kitchen, "There's a lot left."

"Is this okay?" he said as he sat down with a plate of rice and something else. His mother was looking at it. "Fine," she said. I guessed she lived in fear of offending everyone in the family.

"You are my most difficult case," I said, "considering your excellent start in college."

The boy was calmly eating.

I felt I should leave. I had read in Dr. Weil's book, "Avoid the company of agitated minds."

"I should leave," I said.

"Dad will be home from his run," my friend said to her son.

That scared me. He might be grumpy.

Then he entered. It was like a play: "Enter Dad in sweatshirt and pants." He had a worn-out, gym look about him. I pictured a hideous gym with fluorescent lighting.

"Wait till you hear what happened," my friend said. She started to tell about the cake and dog.

"Tell the good part first," I said as I watched her husband getting grumpier.

"He'll be fine because of his weight," she said.

"He'll be fine, but I wanted some chocolate cake," her husband said.

"You can always bake another cake," I said to my friend. I mean, she likes to bake. She's always baking. Or maybe not. Maybe just holidays, and they were over.

"We need the gate," she said.

"He can get the gate; you can bake the cake," I said.

No one seemed happy to hear my idea. My friend looked at me.

Her husband stood in the doorway.

"Look at the present I just got," my friend said to her husband. She took it out of the box and held it up.

"Very . . . cute," he said to us as he looked at it. Any glimmer of hope disappeared from his face as he took in its purity. For a moment he must have hoped it was some other kind of undergarment. He couldn't have been a Victoria's Secret kind of guy, underneath his Ivy League education and high IQ. Maybe he was a La Perla kind of guy, or would have been if he were in the financial top one percentile.

"I'm going to take a shower," he said.

"Well, Happy New Year," I said, although I didn't believe that was possible in the new century.

"Same to you," he said, and left the room.

"COULD YOU clean up the cake mess?" my friend asked her son. "I'm so tired. I can't do *everything!*"

"Okay," he said, and went into the kitchen.

"I cooked and baked for days and days of company. I've done the dog, I've done too much."

"I'm going to leave," I said. "Try to get the gate Monday or ask someone to do it for you."

"Thanks for the undershirt—camisole, really."

"You're welcome. I hope it's the right size."

She walked me to the door. "I'm sure it is. Thank you."

Soon I was on the porch. It was still raining and the dark, wooden porch steps looked slippery. I'd go home to my husband with his fewer demands but his love of TV sports. We had some documentaries from Netflix to watch. *Blind Spot: Hitler's Secretary* was one.

Then I thought of the mittens. I should have mentioned them as I left.

"Thank you for the mittens." That's what I should have said.

GET MONEY

T HE TOWN FELT CRAZY to me as I walked up from Main Street onto the side street. I smelled cigarette smoke and heard a foreign language being screamed out of the church. At first I thought it was a Jamaican Baptist service, then realized the language was Portuguese. An evening performance of some sort was in progress. The church was used for theatrical performances at night.

I was on Nantucket, not in a cosmopolitan city, but it felt the same—the smoke, the high temperature of the late September night, the screaming of the foreign language. Nantucket hadn't always been like that.

In the past, a breeze was always blowing. When asked, I'd give as my first reason for keeping on going there, "I like the way the wind blows."

★ ★ ★

W HERE WAS I going? Nowhere. I had said good-bye to the Jamaican cleaning helper, after handing her as much cash as I
could get from a cash machine. One thing about her—Norma
—that was driving me crazy, among the several things, was the
asking to be paid in cash. I never had cash. Money is dirty, for
one thing—it's filthy. But that's not the main thing.

The main thing wasn't even the important one my mother
had told me when I was six or seven. The subject had to do
with hand-washing and why we should never touch or eat any
food without first washing our hands. Then she told me about
germs and money. She said that she was on the subway and had
seen a drunken bum cough a tubercular-sounding cough into
his hand, and then put his hand on the white metal subway
pole. From my viewpoint, another reason to avoid subways—
from hers, a reason to practice hand-washing.

This led to the second part of her explanation—money.
Drunken derelicts would take those coughed-on, germ-ridden
hands and put them on their money and buy their liquor. The
next, presumably upstanding, person who went into the store
to buy wine or some other higher-class form of alcohol would
be handed back those filthy bills. This was the cycle of money
being passed around town, city, state, and country. After hearing that, I was afraid of touching money.

A couple of decades later, I threw my husband's khakis into
the washing machine with Ecover detergent and Clorox, with-

out knowing that his wallet was in the back pocket. I was surprised to discover—after the spin cycle—fresh, clean green-and-white bills. For the first time, I understood that money was not just paper, but I never bothered to find out exactly what the fiber content was. In childhood, the *Encyclopaedia Britannica Junior*—many volumes of a set of blue books—was in my older sister's room, and she kept me out of there. In this way, there were many things I never learned. Once, she threw a Kleenex box at me when I tried to enter her room. Because the globe was in there, too, I never learned geography of the world.

I did learn late in life that money didn't disintegrate from being washed; it only improved. Money laundering of this kind would be a good idea for our government to try. It's more wholesome than any enterprise in which these officials are presently engaged.

My father had a special method of hand-washing. I would watch him at the sink and then try to copy the technique. He'd arrive home from work. It was during that stage in the life of children—five to seven—when all things are new and fascinating. My father himself seemed fascinating, and his sudden arrival home even more so. Before he did anything else, he would wash his hands. He'd take the soap and lather up his hands and I'd watch as the suds turned dark grey.

In those days, the main brands of soap were Ivory, Palmolive, and a three-inch-thick white oval, Sweetheart. My father would rinse his hands several times and start all over again. The soapsuds would be lighter grey. He'd do this until the suds were white. The white Sweetheart bar turned grey, and that was bad enough, but the grey stuck into the ring of flowers imprinted on the soap and that was even more disturbing to see. But then he washed the soap off, too.

At age five, I gave a review of the soap brands and requested a particular one—Sweetheart. My mother didn't pay attention to the details of the critique but agreed to the request. "Yes, Your Royal Highness," she said.

Palmolive was a dreary green color, and the manufacturer hadn't even tried to get the artificial aroma of flowers of Sweetheart.

I recently saw a bar of Palmolive soap for sale in an antiques store in Rhode Island. It was still in its original, sad green wrapper with the black strip of paper around the middle with the Palmolive name.

Then there was Ivory. It didn't seem to me to be 99.9% pure. It must have been made from animal fat, as almost all soaps were at the time, and that must have accounted for the lack of anything pleasant about it.

After my father rinsed his hands many times, he used a paper towel to dry them. He wasn't a surgeon, just an intellectual man who looked like a movie star, who went to work in an office. He wore a tweed suit and a brown felt hat and rode the subway into Manhattan and back each day.

When I tried out his method and found the grey lather impossible to duplicate, I went to the kitchen and asked my mother, "Why doesn't the soap turn grey?" She said, "It's news-print from reading the *Times* on the subway."

I was surprised because at home he read *The New Republic*, when it was a liberal publication. The pages were rough, but they didn't turn his hands grey.

To prepare for my next hand-washing project, I found a newspaper and tried rubbing it all over the palms of my hands. My mother noticed this activity and asked, "What are you doing, reading *The New York Times?*" I explained that I wanted to get the grey lather. She found this entertaining but continued dinner preparations in her Julia Child–Martha Stewart way while I went to the sink in the bathroom and tried it out.

"It didn't work," I said when I returned to the kitchen. I was disappointed. "Look." I showed her some white suds.

"Daddy reads the paper for half an hour," she said. "He turns all the pages. He folds it and unfolds it and carries it in his hands. You don't want to do that. Go read a book or draw a picture."

T HE MAIN thing was, where to get money? Especially on Nantucket. The two parts, hygiene and location, are connected. Why bring the filthy, bacteria-laden bills into your hand, pocket, wallet, and home when you can use a more hygienic plastic card? The card can be swabbed off with alcohol.

I hadn't been inside a bank since 1989. And good riddance to them—banks and their staff and their décor, so unlike the bank in my favorite Alfred Hitchcock movie, *Shadow of a Doubt*, where Teresa Wright's movie father was employed. She was named Charlotte and called Charlie, after her mother's brother Charles, Joseph Cotten, a murderer. He arrived in town after escaping the detectives on his trail, and moved in with Teresa Wright's movie family, into their big old house on a tree-lined street in Santa Rosa. He slept in her room, and she moved in to share the room of her precocious little sister. I'd read that Alfred Hitchcock searched carefully for just the right American town and house and had filmed this masterpiece on location.

Joseph Cotten wasted no time in going to the bank to deposit money he'd stolen from elderly widows he'd strangled in New York. At this beautiful old bank, he caused an embarrassing scene. Did Joseph Cotten win any well-deserved award for his great and subtle performance in that film? Did anyone know who he was anymore?

I often thought of Paul Shaffer, David Letterman's bandleader and expert on rock and roll. He knew everything. He liked to say, "The kids don't know about these people." He said it smiling with irony and resignation. Those in our generation were no longer regarded as kids.

Money was available at the Stop & Shop, a hellish place best visited only after 10:00 p.m. in summer. There, the angry Jamaican cashiers could give back two hundred dollars above purchase on the bank card. "No cash back," one of them liked to mutter if I arrived after 11:00 p.m., the hour they supposedly emptied the cash drawer.

When the Jamaicans were first brought in to fill the labor gap, they ignored the customers—not even a howdy-do was offered. They stood in casual positions and spoke to each other about personal matters; they spoke in a language Americans couldn't understand. In addition, the language apparently had to be spoken in a loud, urgent tone—a fighting, combative tone—even if the content was amicable and the facial expressions happy. After what must have been many complaints, the employees were trained to stop that behavior and greet customers, "Hello, how are you?"

The first time I heard the greeting, it gave me a jolt. I believe I fell back an inch or so on my old stretched-out, rubber-wedge-soled, straw walking sandals. These leather-free sandals were no longer made, and I was down to my last two pairs. I would stumble, trip, and twist my ankles until Stella McCartney came up with vegan walking sandals.

The supermarket had filthy floors, and a dirty mop, broom, and pail right smack inside the entrance. The white linoleum was always grey with dirt and spilled liquids of unknown origin. Late at night, an employee could be seen sweeping the aisles with a long horizontal-headed dust mop. The mop head was maybe three feet long. The downtrodden man appeared to be from the Communist bloc; younger Bulgarians and other young Eastern bloc-ers were brought in after the polite Irish workers found better jobs at home.

After sweeping a large pile of dust and dirt all the way down the aisles, he would take the mop and shake it into the air and the breathing space of customers who were in the store during the late-evening hours.

I decided to mention this to the store manager. He and I had been on friendly terms since he'd made the effort to order four cases of Panna water—Acqua Panna, the only glass bottles of flat water stocked by the market. "Maybe next week," he'd been saying for a month. Or, "It's on the Cape, we just have to get it over here."

I tried to think of a good way to discuss the shaking-out of the dust-filled mop. After a few minutes, I came up with this sentence formulation: "It would be better if the cleaning crew didn't shake the dust mop into the air."

A Buddhist acquaintance had taught me to phrase all requests in the positive, as he once did in a note on a car windshield: "Please choose a different place to park, as the driveway is in use. Thank you."

The manager answered, "Is that what he's doing? I never see it—I'm in the back with the stock." He promised that he would talk to the fellow.

When I left the store, I couldn't get the sentence out of my mind: "It would be better if the cleaning crew didn't shake the dust mop into the air." If I could have collaborated with Cole Porter, or Paul McCartney, since he was a living songwriter, the sentence could have been part of a song. I'd had other song lyrics in mind for a few years: "You say 'Al Kyda,' I say 'Al Kayda,' Bush says 'nucular,' though he knows it's 'nuclear'" were among the ideas I'd put on hold until I could meet with the great musician.

My husband had told me not to bring up the mop subject with the manager, because his own method was to walk blindly through the downfall of civilization, saying nothing and doing nothing to help remedy the decline experienced by all of us in minor and major ways each day.

That was one of his main character flaws, the others being carnivorism and an overattachment to his original family. The combination of the two or three, or five hundred, was not a good setup for marriage.

I hoped to become financially independent like J. K. Rowling. She was the only woman billionaire I could think of—the only one who'd earned her billions without doing something really bad like hosting daytime TV shows or acting in Hollywood movies. Next I hoped to meet someone like Paul McCartney—like him but without the fame, hair-coloring habit, eyebrow-overgrooming, and psychic damage done by his future ex-wife. Just a vegetarian, musician, animal-rights activist, and garden-lover—a man who lived in the countryside of England or any civilized country.

Which country was a civilized country? Iceland was good, the way they banned dogs in Reykjavik—the only solution to the many problems created by dog owning.

Then there was the extreme case of the island-owning Marlon Brando. I'd always assumed he was a weird guy, but as I learned more about our civilization, I understood that his island owning was the only way to find any peace and quiet.

I'D FIRST gotten the idea about Paul McCartney during the era when I used to watch Craig Ferguson, a Scottish actor-comedian, performing his late-late-night television monologue. This was during the phase when the monologue was filled with wit, knowledge, references to Shakespeare, and once even a rec-itation of several lines from an Elizabeth Barrett Browning sonnet. Perhaps he knew so much because he had been edu-cated in Scotland, not in the United States.

The pronunciation of the word "breadth" in the sonnet was a real surprise—a pleasant surprise—his actor's voice as deep and complicated as Laurence Olivier's. This was before the con-tent of his chatting changed to digestive disturbances and sexual perversion.

At the end of that better era—he was referring to poor Paul McCartney on the day Sir Paul's personal troubles were an-nounced—he'd said in his new, jokey, ageist showbiz style, "Ladies, Paul McCartney's back on the market. Who's inter-ested in a sixty-three-year-old vegetarian?" These may not be his exact words.

I raised my hand, at least mentally. The actor-comedian ap-parently thought vegetarianism was a joke. He had stated before his reason for giving it up—he loved bacon—never having given a thought to the feelings and lives of our intelligent fellow creatures, the pigs.

THE YOUNG Eastern-bloc workers in Nantucket didn't bother to learn much English—even if they bothered, their accents were such that the workers couldn't be understood.

On one occasion, in an out-of-town drugstore, after searching fruitlessly for toothbrushes—the Bulgarians were ignoring me and speaking to each other in their native tongue—I went to the pharmacist in the back. I asked my question concerning the whereabouts of Similasan homeopathic allergy spray, and then mentioned the language problem. The pharmacist was not just over fifty, he was over sixty-five and remembered the past decades of store service and just plain civility in America.

In my favorite Orson Welles movie, *The Stranger,* World War II war-crimes investigator Mr. Wilson—Edward G. Robinson—goes to Connecticut to search for a former top Nazi official, Franz Kindler, who was played by the young, not yet overweight, but still creepy Orson Welles himself.

Mr. Wilson finds there's not much service at the drugstore. The elderly, overweight pharmacist is busy playing checkers and sends the investigator to get a bottle of aspirin down from the shelf on his own. But at least the pharmacist spoke English. He knew the word "aspirin." He discussed the weather. "Looks like it's coming up for snow," he says later on, in a suspense-filled scene.

The Nantucket pharmacist confided that the employees had been told to speak English at work, but they wouldn't comply.

As we discussed the situation, I heard the young Bulgarians speaking in the background—in their native tongue, naturally—and I became more anxious from the sound of the Bulgarian-talking. Then I became aware of these sentences forming in my mind: "This is America. Employees should speak English in the workplace."

I was compelled to say the sentences and then add, "Everyone else did—Italians, Jews, Scandinavians."

"The workplace" was a phrase I never thought I'd say under any circumstances.

The refusal of workers to learn English had caused this new intolerance. At home, in winter, there was an Ecuadorian handyman, who had lived in the United States for ten years without trying to learn even one more word. He knew about ten words, and the number of words never increased. Naturally, this led to mistakes, misunderstandings, wasted time, repeated instructions, and then, madness. In his spare time, instead of learning a few more English words, he bought high-heeled black leather boots, black leather jackets, and gigantic flat-screen TVs. When we offered him a large new Sony TV, which was too big for our small house, he declined, saying, "Too small."

The pharmacist was in agreement about the language issue, but with a guilty look. I asked, "May I pay for the toothbrushes here, or do I have to go back down to Bulgaria?" He smiled and accepted payment. "I don't mean to sound like Patrick Buchanan," I said as an apology.

"He's getting more liberal," the pharmacist said with enthusiasm.

THE JAMAICAN cleaning helper was going back to her country for a week to see her family. Her full-time job was working at a big, expensive hotel on the ocean. The hotel kept her employed from April to November but her teenaged children needed her. She was worried about one of them, whose minor medical symptoms she liked to describe every time she came to work.

When she did this describing, I thought of a wealthy neighbor who had a Ukrainian housekeeper who neither spoke nor understood English. These Ukrainians can be so scary that meeting just one or two of them enables a complete understanding of the Cold War. I realized that meeting just a few people from other countries can lead to a better grasp of world history. Learning this history in high school didn't seem interesting or pertinent compared to rock and roll.

I'd recently heard a Ukranian or Russian—a big, Soviet-looking expert—explaining how the poisoned Prime Minister of the Ukraine could have eaten soup without tasting the dioxin that almost killed him and did disfigure his face. "It was thick borscht—with garlic, onions, cabbage, turnips, kale," the expert said in his thick accent, which made the soup sound even thicker. The explanation was that with all these healthful, strong flavors of vegetables, with spices, too, the Prime Minister might not have noticed the dioxin. Now that was interesting. And the recipe sounded good—minus the poison. I wanted to try it out if the weather ever turned cold.

When I asked the wealthy neighbor—since she was a nouveau I had no fear of asking—how she managed with the foreign-language communication problem, she said that it was exactly what she wanted—no conversations with housekeepers. "I don't want to hear about their gynecological problems and their family tragedies." I guessed she had a point. I asked how she gave instructions for housekeeping tasks. "I show them—I act it out," she said.

After I knew her well enough to be asked into her house, I did see her speaking a kind of pig Latin, or pig Russian, to the Ukrainian housekeeper. I knew the country of origin only because I'd been told, "She can sleep in the storage room—she's from the Ukraine, she doesn't care."

Although I couldn't believe anyone would say this sentence, I still decided to ask her about some conservation land in Connecticut, near where she lived in winter. She said she didn't know anything about the land. I persisted in trying to find out about it. She became more and more impatient and finally said, "Don't you understand I don't care about anything that doesn't affect me personally?" Then, due to shock and disbelief, I said nothing.

I had the opposite kind of relationship with any part-time helpers who came to our rented cottage. Forced by empathy and fear of seeming impolite, I listened to whole life stories. And back at our own winter house I had the great fortune to have the part-time help of a tiny, intelligent Japanese woman— the woman who told me that when she first came to this country she couldn't believe that "American people" used white vinegar for salad dressing, or as any edible ingredient. One day, she came to work with this news: "I learned how to prepare Kukicha tea by roasting old green tea in a pan. It's fun," she said.

This woman was more interesting than any of my friends. Why was she dusting and vacuuming for a living? It would be rude to ask. I'd detected that much from her Japanese etiquette.

She drank coffee from a thermos all day, and when I gave her some organic coffee beans, she mentioned that she'd received a gift of coffee from one of her other clients.

"One was Upper-West-Side Blend, the other was SoHo Blend," she said. We both laughed at that. I asked how the coffee blends were. She looked up from her chore of dusting and said, "Upper-West-Side was not good, but SoHo Blend was tasty." We started to laugh again, and I was afraid that we weren't going to be able to stop.

She was always learning new things. She liked to knit, crochet, and sew in her free time when she wasn't cooking miso soup and seaweed broth, recipes she described and tried to teach me.

She instructed me to throw out the packages of certain kinds of seaweed in the pantry, explaining that they were too old to be used. Nori didn't keep long; wakame, hiziki, and kombu were okay to keep longer. Then, one day she wrote me a note about a jar of a sesame seed, seaweed, and salt combination:

> We Japanese do not keep these or any
> other kind of sprinkles so long.
> We usually finish in 2 to 3 weeks because
> we eat them with rice,
> and we eat rice a lot.
> Moisture ruin the taste
> and flavor.
>
> See you next week.

I remembered a discussion the year before, when she'd complained about her nightly cooking routine: "Rice rice rice, rice rice rice," she'd said.

It was white rice, too. She'd said the Japanese don't use brown rice, and I didn't want to see the picture of the pot of white rice in my mind.

She said that she liked to watch the Korean news because it was the most interesting news program. The Koreans respected their elders, she said. For example, if a young Korean person wanted to smoke a cigarette, he or she would wait for the elders to start smoking first. Not a great example, I thought.

She and her husband smoked full-time. All her clothes absorbed the cigarette smoke, and when she arrived for work she had to change and leave the cigarette-smelling ones in a box in the mudroom before entering the house.

The Japanese, she'd said, had become Westernized and were picking up bad American habits. That was the reason she was learning the Korean language from TV subtitles, "just for a hobby."

She would sometimes tell me a fact or two about Japanese culture, which I understood to be superior to ours in almost every way, sexism being the exception. While she was putting some Mozart piano concerto CDs into their rightful cases she said, "In Japan, Vladimir Ashkenaz is very famous. People are so happy that he is there." She didn't pronounce the y and I didn't correct her. In fact, it sounded better without the y. We examined his photo on the CD cover. "I recognize him," she said.

"But he looks different now," I said, looking at the youthful pianist in the picture.

"Yes," she said. "He looks different."

SHE SAID that she would take our old washing machine, which was rusting and disintegrating. We had to replace it, even though we didn't like replacing any appliance, since the old ones were better made. The appliances in my dollhouse from the nineteen-fifties looked so much better than the new real ones manufactured now. The hours required to figure out which one out of hundreds to order—these hours are a waste of your life. Everything was easier when there was a choice of three.

The helper had an even older, rustier machine that she kept fixing herself. When she told the part about fixing it herself, I decided to give her a new machine as a present—a basic model cost about $400. But when I tried to arrange a delivery date with her, she declined, saying she wouldn't feel right about accepting a new machine.

"There is one thing I would rather have, and it is so precious to me," she said. She clasped her hands over her heart as she spoke. I asked what it was, although I was afraid she might say a $10,000 loan. Instead she said, "It is your book, *Marilyn,* you keep under the couch. I love Marilyn Monroe so much. Especially before she was a movie star."

I was surprised. "I didn't know that," I said. "I love her, too." I didn't keep the book under there by any kind of plan—it was too big to fit into the bookshelf.

"In Japan, many peoples are so interested in her," she said. "To me, Marilyn Monroe is the loveliest woman in the world."

We retrieved the book from underneath the couch and studied some of the photos.

"Look how sweet she is," the Japanese helper said. "She is so beautiful."

I looked at the photo. It had been taken before any minor cosmetic work had been done to the actress's face—her chin added onto a little and her nose cartilage thinned out a bit. We compared the photos.

"See, this was done to her nose," I said, touching the photo.

"Oh, I didn't know that," the helper said.

"You know, in my childhood, lots of teenaged girls looked like this," I said. "The babysitter, the neighbor."

"The girl next door?" she said, trying out an American phrase she'd learned.

"Some girls," I said. I pictured those girls and remembered how my mother tried to discourage my childhood attempts to copy their style.

I didn't tell her that my mother referred to the looks of these kinds of girls as cheap. And especially about Marilyn Monroe—she'd once said, "Just another slut." I was only eight at the time, but sensed this was something bad.

"Many women are beautiful, but only a few are lovely. Marilyn Monroe was the loveliest of all," the tiny helper said. "She had inside beauty."

I agreed. I didn't want to get carried away thinking about Marilyn Monroe and her tragic life. I saw through the window that this was the best part of the day. The winter light was slanting onto the trees, two cardinals were at the bird feeder, and I knew that thinking about Marilyn was a downward path. I wanted to get outside and these kinds of conversations always prevented me from leaving.

"I'll get you a new copy," I said. "But you need a washing machine."

"No, please, if I need a machine my husband will agree," she said. "But I could not spend money on a book of young photos of Marilyn Monroe."

BECAUSE I was feeling sorry about the plight of the Jamaican helper—working double or triple shifts at the hotel, walking a mile in the globally-warmed-up summer heat to work at our house on her days off, sleeping in a dormitory room with two other employees, having to fly to Jamaica and back—I offered to go with her to town at 8:00 p.m. the night before her trip, and get her some cash from the bank machine.

The machine was inside a doorway entrance to the bank. There was no air in the entranceway and the temperature was always ninety to a hundred degrees. In a cash emergency before this one I had tried keeping the door open with my foot while I stretched the distance to the machine to perform the nerve-racking transaction.

It's important to avoid touching the buttons on the machine. They've been touched thousands of times, and the withdrawal button is always worn down more than the deposit button. My method was to use the corner of the card to punch in my code.

This takes some manual dexterity and leg stretching, but even without as many yoga classes as I needed, I managed the long stretch to the machine. It would be difficult to explain to the next person, who was sure to come along, the kind of person who doesn't mind absence of air during cash-machine transactions, transportation, and exercise classes. The list of hot, airless places is long.

I told Norma that I would get the cash if she would hold the door open. She agreed, with that little smile of thinking that the desire for air was craziness.

Another thing she couldn't grasp was vegetarianism. Our first dispute involved the vegetarian topic. I told her she might like to have her lunch outside on the screened porch, where she would have fresh air and a view of the small garden. She often said she loved Nantucket and liked to look at anything outside. But I never suggested that she cook up packaged, dehydrated meat soup in the oven. This is what happened once when I came into the kitchen:

"What is that?" I asked. I tried to keep the hysteria down.

"It's just some noodle soup I put into the microwave." She was looking at that horrid invention, the radioactive wall oven.

"We don't ever use that," I said. "It gives off radiation."

"Everyone has them," she said. "I just cooked up the soup."

"Let me see the package," I said. I forgot to add "please."

"It's just turk soup. It's all noodles," she said.

"It's not," I said. "I can tell."

I took the container and read the label. Just as I suspected, lard and chicken were among the main ingredients. I showed her. "I didn't realize that," she said. "In Jamaica, we all like this."

"This is a vegetarian kitchen," I said. "No animal food comes in here."

"I took it outside to eat," she said.

"You can't bring it to cook in here—it's a product of the slaughterhouse. Here, take this," I said. I opened the kitchen cabinet and handed her a cup of Fantastic Chicken-Free Vegetarian Noodle Soup.

"I can't eat American-type soup," she said. She looked at it with suspicion.

"Have some fruit from the refrigerator. Have anything in there you like," I said. I knew that organically grown fruit, nuts, vegetables, and Ezekiel organic sprouted-grain bread were the only things in there.

She'd said before that she liked melon and apples, but she had a fear of the organically grown. Bottles of organically grown fruit juice—pomegranate, peach, blueberry, cranberry— were off limits for her.

If she brought that up, I didn't know what I'd do. I'd been cutting down on the Xanax and was likely to lose control. She gave me the look, and agreed to have some melon even though she didn't "really like cantaloupe." She liked only what she described as "that red melon."

"You mean watermelon?" I asked, and she said yes. I didn't like hearing this because of the racial stereotypes—racist jokes, cartoons, rag dolls, carvings, pictures, and the history of all other kinds of slurs. And how was I going to get a gigantic watermelon home and into the refrigerator, just for a serving for one person?

A worse cooking incident occurred shortly after this one.

"What's that?" I asked as I noticed the fresh air missing from the kitchen.

"It's just lunch from the staff cafeteria," she said, putting a defiled-looking fork into the sink.

"It's a product of the slaughterhouse."

I thought of Paul McCartney having been voted the most popular vegetarian in England. I'd read about his requirement that even his employees had to be vegetarian—so much easier to find in the British employment pool. Incidents of this kind would be avoided.

I'd also read on the Paul McCartney Google Alert that after an angry scene with his future ex-wife, the servants came in to find broken tableware and furniture, and "vegetarian" food spilled all over the floor. Why did the word "vegetarian" have to be added? "Food" would have been sufficient to describe the picture. I imagined the kind of menu that had provoked someone to describe it that way. Did it include red quinoa, green soybeans, or millet loaf? These are some of the foods that can disturb people the most.

I thought I could tell from our conversations that Norma had an average IQ. But she couldn't understand the way I showed her things to do. She reminded me of a part-time clerical assistant who helped, or hindered, me in the winter.

Both of these "helpers" moved slowly and looked perturbed by any new idea or word. Born in the United States, the clerical one had been poorly educated here. But neither of these grown women, one forty-four, the other fifty-four, could understand simple directions. The clerical hinderer was an all-American nitwit. Even ordinary words were new to her. She loved to pronounce words wrong, even when she was looking at them right on an envelope. I wasn't sure she could read.

In Norma's case, maybe she was simply overtired from her real job working at the hotel all day. The word "radiation" was new to her.

She believed that if she handled something cold after something hot, she would catch a cold. She couldn't touch the refrigerator after ironing—this was an absolute rule. I assumed it was part of Jamaican superstition and stopped arguing after I tried to explain the cold virus.

When she dusted the blinds, she would pull them up and leave them up no matter how hot the sun was beating in on the window. I told her that as the sun moved around we could open them. "Sun is heat," I tried to teach her.

"If it's dark, spiders will come," a former Jamaican helper had told me when I explained this method of shade. Because her name was Hyacinth, I always remembered the conversation.

Norma wouldn't close the door when she went out to the porch for the chores she did as slowly as she possibly could. The sun and heat would quickly come pouring into the one air-conditioned room. She couldn't understand that if light cotton rag rugs were walked on with outside shoes, they would turn dark grey. But the most serious was her failure to comprehend that any artistic endeavor was work. My work was to photograph the light as it lit up the morning, the afternoon, and the evening.

Another part of the project was to photograph the weather— the second reason for being on Nantucket. First it could be cloudy and foggy, then bright and sunny, then dark and stormy, then cloudy to partly cloudy, ending with golden light and twilight—the color in Magritte's paintings titled *L'Empire des lumières* and *Le Seize septembre*. All this in one day or even an hour. Only the new never-ending heat and humidity of July and August weren't worth photographing, unless the subject was surrealism.

When I'd mentioned the Magritte sky to a fifth-generation Nantucketer, even before he was a real estate broker, he'd said, "Magritte! You have to have a house here!" He'd studied art history in college. Most people he knew came to Nantucket for other reasons: the hipness, cocaine, music bars, and romantic relationships—the last, a euphemism.

I tried to stay inside between 11:00 and 2:00 but then I found the sun getting hot by 10:00 a.m., then by 9:00 a.m., and staying hot until first 3:00, then 4:00, then 5:00. If Norma was working on anything in the house during any of those hours she would assume I did nothing but stay inside, brewing green tea, doing yoga, taking showers, and listening to her philosophy of life. Photographs and books all over the house didn't signify work to her. They signified nothing. She treated me as if I were Marlene Dietrich in *Morocco*—the parts without the cabaret act.

This might have been caused by seeing and ironing my white

linen shirts and skirts, similar in style to the costume the actress wore in the last scene when she kicks off her high-heeled shoes and follows Gary Cooper into the desert with the troops of the Foreign Legion. Her clothes look like silk, the wrong fabric choice for the climate of Morocco, in which the characters complain about the heat, and are fanning themselves in the very first scene and all the way through to the end of the film.

When Norma came across a photo I had kept from this last scene in *Morocco,* she asked, "Is that your mom? Or grand-mother?"

"You mean Marlene Dietrich?" I said, and she said, "Your mom was Marlene? I didn't think you ever told me that."

I tried explaining who the actress was, and then I felt all tired out.

I thought about a photo of my mother on the deck of the *Île de France,* before she came back to the United States, got married, and lost everything to motherhood and housekeeping. In the photo, she was dressed the way Marlene Dietrich was in the scene before the last, when she searches for and finds Gary Cooper alive and drunk in a bar. Both glamorous women—the actress and my mother—wore what appeared to be white or beige trench coats and tight, cloche-style hats. My mother had bought the hat in Paris but told us that the country of origin was Morocco. I imagined her in her youth—perhaps inspired by the actress in the film *Morocco*—dressed similarly and lolling about on a wooden deck chair on the ocean liner, circa 1938.

"My mother was taller and had a better figure," I said. "And her legs were thinner and perfectly shaped."

She used to tell us that Marlene Dietrich's legs had been insured for a huge sum, like a million dollars—huge at that time, a pittance today. My mother must have been thinking that luck and chance had put the actress in that better situation and left my mother pursuing Martha Stewart's perfect-home interests, without the benefit of wealth—never-ending household drudgery and childcare.

"So your mom was a movie star," Norma said. "I see your resemblance, too, taller and more narrow."

"We don't have the facial bone structure," I said.

In childhood, I thought that my mother looked like Ava Gardner or when she was angry, Joan Crawford in her earliest films. She'd never tweeze her eyebrows in the style of Marlene Dietrich.

Her eyebrows were high enough without any tricks, and mine were so high that my husband had described my eyes as lizard-eyes. When he had the poor judgment to point this out to my mother, she said, "Don't you know that's desirable? Look at the Italian Renaissance paintings." I explained this eyebrow situation to Norma, minus the Renaissance paintings.

"Who are those other names you said? I haven't heard about the old-time stars," she added as an extra blow.

"I'll tell you later," I said, showing her some details of the photo of Marlene Dietrich.

"See, her clothes are silk and they drape and flutter in the desert wind. Mine are just wrinkled linen."

"You should get some new clothes," she said. "Get these, like your mom's in the photo in the desert."

OTHER TIMES she was sensible and offered good advice. "You know, us women, we all have the same kind of problems with men," she'd say on a day when we had time to talk for a few minutes. Or, "Don't stress yourself out about dust mites. Look at the beautiful Nantucket we both love."

JUST AS I'd be leaving to catch the light and saying good-bye, please don't vacuum near the room where my husband is sleeping after his five-mile run in the noonday sun, Norma would suddenly ask to be paid her salary for the week or month.

"What's the amount?" I'd ask.

"I didn't have the time to do it," she'd say.

"Why don't you do it when you first get here?"

"To tell you the truth, it just slipped my mind. I can do it now."

Things were always slipping her mind. But something she always had in mind was that I'd wait while she did the math, partly by counting on her fingers—nothing wrong with that method, as a rule, but the sun would start to get lower and everything I needed for my photos would be disappearing.

Her first preference, which she'd tried before, was to have us both stand there while she named the days and hours. She expected me to add these up. "Monday . . . no, Tuesday. Or was it Sunday? I worked three hours . . . or two and a half hours. Then, Wednesday, I had two shifts at the hotel and I worked one and a half hours." She liked to list all her cleaning activities and how long they would take. At last, I'd get out, I'd rush back at the agreed hour, and she still wouldn't have done the addition.

"You add it up and give it to me," I'd say. "Whatever it is, it's fine. I can't stand and add."

I tried offering her a deposit on account, but she always had a reason why she needed the whole amount—while I was in the doorway—a crazy reason, too. It would be a reason like, "I have to buy some earrings in Hyannis for a birthday present. I have to take the early boat over and back tomorrow."

"I'm going to miss the light," I'd say. I'd be feeling a panic starting because missing the light reminded me of everything I'd missed in life.

R IGHT OFF the bat, I had asked Norma to dress for work, not for leisure, but she had only two sets of hotel-work clothes and she had to scrub them hard every night. This picture and these words were so pitiful that I offered to buy her another set but she said no. The truth was she liked to come to our house dressed in the style of the times, as a slatternly wench—a forty-

four-year-old wench. The bottom of the costume consisted of
tight blue jeans, stretched even tighter in that Lycra denim over
her wide thighs.

On top she dared to wear a half-on-half-off-the-shoulder
black and metallic, fuchsia striped T-shirt. For her footwear she
chose rhinestone thong sandals. "This is my day off, so I wear
these clothes," she'd said.

"But you're working."

"It's not the hotel, so I like to wear these."

"It's right to dress for work in work clothes," I said.

I didn't like the way delivery men and service men looked at
her dressed in her leisure outfits and I knew this could be cur-
tailed by the hotel uniform. I was right because although I'd
seen them show interest when women were in these uniforms,
the interest was more polite and less lascivious. The day-off
outfit brought out the big smile, then the chatting, then the
loud laughing, then moving on to loud talking in the Jamaican
language. Finally, we agreed on her wearing khaki slacks and
any of the shirts she liked.

ON THIS evening, after getting a wad of cash from the bank
machine, we walked across the street together.

"Be careful," she said, looking at my stretched, rubber-
wedged straw sandals. "You need sneakers for these cobble-
stones. Why don't they replace these cobbles with regular
streets?"

"History," I told her. "History of Nantucket." "Oh," she said. But she didn't want to know what that meant and I didn't want to tell her.

It would be good if the foreign employees, when trained for work, were shown a film on Nantucket history. Tourists would benefit from the film as well. Both groups now thought it was just a resort, not an island of history, and they behaved in accordance with this notion.

Norma was wearing one of her glamorous wigs, which she referred to as "hair extensions."

"Because I don't always have time to relax my hair," she explained.

I once asked why she couldn't just let it be natural, and she said, "I can't stand that."

I guessed she didn't know who Charlayne Hunter-Gault was, so I didn't mention her name. "What about Whitney Houston?" I asked.

"Whitney Houston? She's terrible."

"But her hair looks good," I said.

Norma shook her head.

"How about Diana Ross?" I said.

"Diana Ross—she's terrible, too."

"But her hair is nice. She looks beautiful," I said. I didn't mention the Supremes' songs I used to listen to during an era of history and life that was so much more fun than the present one.

"No, I like the extensions," she said. "They're better for me."

This wig was her most glamorous, with long bangs and a

small ponytail. In bright light, I saw gold and maroon streaks. The construction material looked like the kind used for modern dolls' wigs, wigs even less realistic than my Toni doll's wig from the nineteen-fifties. In childhood, the nature of the shininess was so unrealistic that I could stare at the doll's hair for hours.

The first time Norma removed her wig in the house, I saw that her partially relaxed hair was only three inches long and stood up all over as if a strong wind had blown it, or the way comic-book characters looked when they'd been frightened—a fashionable style with rock stars and with others now. I understood her predicament.

I asked why she didn't let it grow and then uncurl it into the same style as the wig. I wanted to use the word "straighten" but was afraid it had a racial connotation. The other word, "relaxed," was in the same category as the new usage of the word invented for phonying-up fabric or paint finishes on furniture to be fake antique—"distressed." I'd never use it with that meaning, and if anyone said it to me I had to quickly turn away from the person.

"Oh no, it would take so long—two years to grow it," she said.

THE EVENING of the cash expedition, she said she hoped to get her dinner at the staff cafeteria. One day I asked what was served and she said all kinds of food, Jamaican food and regular American food. I asked what the Jamaican food was and she said, "Oh, rice, beans, vegetables, jerked chicken." One thing I never wanted to know was the definition of jerked animal products of any kind. The other thing I wanted to know even less was the meaning of the more disgusting-sounding "pulled pork." I asked what the American food was, and she said, "Oh, spaghetti and things like that. Potatoes."

"Is all the food in the same area?" I asked.

"Oh, yes, we all eat together. The whites . . ."

I thought she was about to describe the color of the American food but she was talking about race distinction. "The whites have their food and the Jamaicans have theirs—but they can eat together. Whatever they want."

On this one occasion of getting the cash without visiting the supermarket, Norma and I stood on Main Street in front of the drugstore saying good-bye for quite a while. I asked whether it was a good idea for her to work so hard and then have to fly home to see her psychosomatic daughter. She said it was necessary.

"I have to send money home," she said. I asked whether it wouldn't be better to have less money and more time with her family. "I care about having a nice home," she said. "My dream is to buy a house overlooking the water in a peaceful, beautiful place. That's what I want."

"Don't we all," I said. "But it's impossible. We can't even buy a little house outside of town, miles from the water."

"You have to," she said. "After all these years—your whole life almost—you have to own a house in Nantucket."

That was one of her other things that was driving me crazy.

"Go talk to a real estate broker," she'd say, "I've seen pictures in the paper."

And I'd say, "I don't have three million dollars." All she could say was, "Three million dollars?"

She thought that real estate brokers were actual human beings, that you could ask a question and get a true answer. I'd talked to one of these brokers, one I'd known for thirty years, when we were really young and he was still a regular person. This was before he was trained to be one of them, the way people were regular humans before being transformed inside giant pods in *The Invasion of the Body Snatchers*.

In his real-estate-viewing car, when I admired his shirt, he said, "Just L.L. Bean."

I told him I'd heard that they were a conservative right-wing company. He was surprised. "They can keep their goddamn boots!" he said. He had retained his sense of humor and political viewpoint, having lost his soul to the real estate business, or in a pod.

Then, in this fun frame of mind, we went driving around looking at run-down junk for sale in chain-link-fenced areas. The price range—one to two million. As I got out of his car and waved a demoralized good-bye, he called, "Get money."

I ASKED Norma the price of her dream house in Jamaica and she said $400,000.

"You can't earn that vacuuming at the hotel," I said. "You have to buy a Powerball lottery ticket."

"Gambling is against my religion."

"What if I bought it for you?" I thought of the places I would have to go to purchase such a thing—a lottery ticket. It wasn't possible. My husband had often suggested lottery tickets for over twenty years as a means to buy a cottage in Nantucket. And I'd driven by the lottery ticket places with him but always waited in the car. He had this in his head, instead of any realistic plans to help us live on the once peaceful island. And now the past decades of peace and quiet in Nantucket were gone. Building, hammering, nail guns shooting, chain saws, jackhammers, power mowers, motorcycles, trucks, and boombox cars were among the sounds replacing birds singing.

"I don't know if I could accept money won from the lottery," Norma said.

During my childhood, there was an Orthodox Jewish family who used to ask us to turn their lights on during the Sabbath. Would it be the same kind of thing?

"Well, it's just a fantasy," I said. "We're in the same boat."

"No, don't say that," she said. "I'm going to pray for you."

"Don't pray for real estate," I said. "God isn't involved in real estate. Pray for world peace."

I thought of that scene Steve Martin did, maybe in the nineteen-seventies, when the mentioning of world peace wasn't a terrible joke. First he'd wish for all the selfish, materialistic, immoral things he wanted for himself. This was funny. Then he'd remember world peace, start over, and add that on—in first place. That was funny, too.

"People have no place to live," I said. "They live in tents in the frozen hills of Pakistan and on the filthy streets of Bangladesh."

I didn't mention Africa. I knew I'd panic when I pictured it. Then, the OTHER: I saw the word in my mind, beginning with "I," ending with "q." I wasn't going to say it. The sound of the word was like a weapon. The middle part was harsh and the sound seemed to now contain everything horrible happening there. Then the letters "ACK," the identifying initials for the Nantucket airport, were in complete fun-contrast to that situation. Some people had ACK bumper stickers on their cars and when overdevelopment and traffic began to ruin Nantucket, one man created the bumper sticker "ICK." Unfortunately, the stickers weren't for sale.

Norma acted as though the world situation was news to her—after spending her free time reading the *Globe,* the *Midnight Sun,* and the *Enquirer,* then watching *Hollywood Insider* on TV. I didn't expect she'd be watching the *BBC World News* or *Euro-News,* but I thought she might know a bit about all this.

If there was a great headline, I'd buy her one of those magazines, which she referred to as books: "Bill Clinton Mentally Ill," or "Laura to Divorce George." The greatest I'd ever seen—"Hitler Was Jewish," to say nothing of the accompanying "article"—that would be beyond her.

"I'm going to pray for you anyway," she said.

"No. Please," I said. "If you win a lottery ticket, you can give to charity."

"That's true," she said. "Well, I better get some dinner and go back home and pack up for the early-morning boat."

I would have asked her to dinner in the hipster diner, but she'd told me many times that she couldn't eat American food.

"They have rice and beans there, too," I'd told her. What I didn't tell her was that these foods were fava beans and basmati rice. That would have scared her.

"But not the Jamaican style," she'd said.

I imagined going in there together. She would be nervous—the only Jamaican dining. Even the workers weren't Jamaican. The owners hadn't yet used up the Brazilian and Portuguese resources. The dishwasher and his wife worked at several jobs and had bought a house for only $780,000 when the prices were still low.

I LOOKED at Norma dressed in her hotel uniform, an egalitarian-looking choice of khaki slacks and a white polo shirt with a collar in the style of the first Lacoste polo shirts. She could have been a hotel guest, except for the small insignia of the hotel name and symbol on the shirt. How could guests be distinguished from housekeeping staff? No problem—race was the key: all the guests white, all the help Jamaican. When I first walked by the hotel and saw the Jamaican bellmen and door-

men outside on the porch, all wearing the same kind of uniform—khaki pants and white polo shirts—I was reminded of a
plantation in *Gone With the Wind*.

"Let's get out of here," I'd said to my husband.

" I HOPE you have a good trip," I said to Norma.

A middle-aged tourist couple was sitting on a bench nearby.
They were looking at us and smiling. Maybe they were thinking what a racially advanced state Massachusetts was—compared to Mississippi anyway. Maybe they were just talking
about getting some ice cream before the drugstore counter
closed. Grown-ups of all ages could be seen on Main Street
eating ice cream, apparently without any vision of their arteries
plaquing up.

I put my hand on Norma's shoulder and kissed her good-
bye. This made her give that little smile. In this case, I wasn't
sure what it meant.

CRAMP BARK

I N ORDER TO DISTRACT my mind from the whole world
situation, I decided to walk down the street to the bookstore. In the beautiful evening, or night, the bookstore stayed
open until the exemplary hour of 10:30 p.m. It was the only
game in town. I'd heard of a psychiatrist who had admitted that
psychotherapy was not that great, but said, "It's the only game
in town." The bookstore was that great. In addition to books,
they sold mints named "Impeachmints," in a tin with Bush's so-
called face; another, "National Embarrassmints," with the
same; and my favorite, "Indictmints," with the whole group in
striped jail uniforms. There was also a Van Gogh action figure
I'd been considering all summer, and I was ready to make these
purchases. Since my husband was away there was no one to
stop me.

On my way down the block, I saw that there was no line outside the restored diner-luncheonette and I could go in.

The regular hostess was a graduate student from Boston and she'd mentioned that she was a vegetarian. When I'd told her I was a vegan, she said, "Me, too." The immediate bond created, we compared notes on how to get the sous-chef to deconstruct the menu for us.

"Now you have someone on the inside," the sous-chef said to me when he overheard our conversation.

In September, classes started for the vegan hostess, and other young women had to fill in. I knew one of them from the bookstore where she worked at one of her three or four jobs. This fill-in hostess had told me that she was nervous about managing three seatings. "Come back and see what happens," she'd said.

When I came back, the tables were filled with happy-looking couples and screaming, wine-drinking gangs of six. I thought I'd sit down at the front of the counter near the door and order some Panna water. The water was the one thing I could count on not having touched any animal product in preparation or on the grill.

At the other end of the counter, I saw the fill-in hostess sitting down and dining. She waved to me as if I were a normal person other people wave to. I went along with it and walked down to say hello.

Then I saw that her dining companion was the Brigitte Bardot girl, a thirty-two-year-old woman whose main interests in life were fashion and looking good. This girl never wanted to talk to me, I assumed, because I was over forty-nine and she thought my days of style were in the past.

Every day I wore the same thing—a straight linen skirt and a plain linen camisole with a linen camp shirt on top of it. I had twelve of each, all white or beige. The local doctor, a forty-nine-year-old woman, had said to me, "You're always in your white linen shirts, I guess from some elegant store in New York."

"No, L.L. Bean," I said. This was before I'd been told that L.L. Bean was a conservative Republican company and I'd switched to Lands' End. "I never go to New York."

"How can anyone live in that filthy city?" the doctor said.

"My husband keeps me a prisoner only a hundred miles away so that he can go back and forth."

I noticed that the physically fit–looking doctor dressed in slinky slacks and thin cotton sweaters.

ONE EVENING when the Brigitte girl was filling in for the fill-in hostess—anyone who looked good could be hired—I admired her jacket. "It's vintage," she said in a haughty way. Even though I was one of the first to buy antique clothing in the nineteen-seventies, I didn't want to say, "I bought antique clothing before you were born."

That wouldn't have the effect I wanted. I knew "vintage" was now used to mean anything old—even something from the eighties. More evidence of the lack of education in the new, decadent, lazy generation.

When the Brigitte girl had once told me a name of a designer from the nineteen-eighties, after first saying "vintage," I'd said, "What vintage is that? He's a living, working person with his own name." She didn't bother to answer.

Whenever I'd thought of giving the Nantucket Thrift Shop any of my antique clothes, I'd imagine this girl getting hold of them and I couldn't go through with the donation.

In retrospect, I realized that I should have given them all directly to her, in a turn-the-other-cheek gesture I hadn't yet mastered.

When I first saw the Brigitte girl, I knew she was unusual looking. She looked good in the Brigitte Bardot way. Her face was a bit puffy from what I assumed to have been nights of debauchery that are common in her generation—alcohol, smoking, and other substances. I didn't know enough about the subject to be sure which ones caused puffiness. If she didn't watch out, she was going to find herself looking like Simone Signoret.

The fill-in hostess sometimes said that Brigitte was beautiful, and I had to inform her: "Yes, but not enough bone structure for lasting looks." I didn't mention Simone Signoret, fearing the question, "Who's that?" I couldn't possibly explain the movie *Diabolique,* and I didn't want to pronounce it correctly in French, stuck as I was to my childhood pronunciation—Dyeab-o-leek—and all the fun times that went with the title.

No world-history education, okay, I'd accepted this about her generation, but film history at least would have been fun for them.

She was wearing tight, Bermuda-length blue jeans which looked fine because she had long, thin legs and her legs and arms and face were naturally tan. She didn't have a tan, she had tan skin, the kind of skin that doesn't show veins or freckles or capillaries as time marches on.

With these Bermuda jeans she was wearing a scandalous-looking shoulderless black-lace sweater, a fashion incongruity I guessed she'd picked up reading *Vogue* and watching runway fashion shows on TV.

She had the runway walk, or a slighter version of it, when she walked through the restaurant's narrow corridor between the small tables and the counter.

She leaned over the counter and said something to the chef, who had a well-known weakness for women and girls of all kinds and ages. This weakness showed on his overheated, red face.

I saw that I was going to be in my mother's shoes, crushed by the next generation's view of us as nobodies—not just as past our prime, but as never having had a prime.

The way I'd met the Brigitte girl was through our mutual friend, the actor-waiter with the dangerously over-tanned skin, super-bleached white teeth, and platinum-blond hair. He'd told me a few years before that the Brigitte girl was his best friend. Luckily, I hadn't said anything against her.

He referred to her by her real name, Jayne, and when I didn't
know who she was he said, "You know, the one who comes in
here. She's very stylish and great looking. She wears Bermuda-
length jeans and glittery sweaters. She has long light brown hair
and a permanent tan. She looks like a model."

"Is it the Brigitte Bardot girl?" I asked.

"Is that what you call her?" he said with his big white smile.
"It must be the same one. She'd be so happy."

"She doesn't look like a model," I said. "She looks like a real
person."

"Well, she tries to look like a model. She's always calling me
up late at night and asking me to come right over and color her
hair the way some model has it in *Vogue*. She reads fashion magazines every spare minute she has."

"I didn't know she was your best friend," I said.

"We met in New York, working in a store on Madison
Avenue and then in restaurants downtown."

I remembered that she'd said in her faux-snobby way that
she'd been coming to Nantucket her whole life. I'd said I'd been
coming before her life began, but she appeared to think that the
years spent by people in Nantucket before her lifetime was time
that didn't count. It just meant the people were older than
those in her generation, and they didn't count either.

She was one of the ones who sat smoking on the benches on
Main Street. I was always surprised to see an attractive young
person smoking. What reason could any of them have? When
I'd recently seen her on the bench she was wearing a heavy

jacket, though the date was still late, hot September. She was the kind who couldn't wait to get into her new black winter garments, even though winter was slow in coming and fall never quite got under way, the extra-long summer having begun in full force that year.

She'd once told me the name of a designer. I'd never heard of him. She said that he'd worked with Karl Lagerfeld, whom I presumed to be the only really old person she respected.

I knew about this kind of thinking because I'd heard the forty-four-year-old Jon Stewart make a joke about Mick Jagger and say that the Rolling Stones were old. That was a cruel blow. The Rolling Stones will never be old. Even a hundred years from now. The same goes for Paul McCartney.

I HAD been to her place of daytime employment only once. It was an expensive, trampy clothing store. The visit was during the heyday of the style of prostitute-clothes-for-all. I'd admired her sweater when we'd met at the diner-restaurant, where she was sitting at the counter after working as the hostess for the evening. It was short-sleeved, with a crocheted pattern knitted into it all over. An undergarment was necessary for modesty, and, to her credit, she wore one. The sweater had a turtleneck, which I was planning to have removed if I found one in my size. She said she didn't wear turtlenecks, either, but had made an exception for this particular sweater. It was a pale-peach color and the kind I'd bought before the stage of life where clingy open-knit sweaters no longer seemed appropriate. I'd asked her about it in a moment of denial and regression, the kind of moment that had resulted in my mother's closet being filled with knitwear she could never wear.

The sweater had been sold out even before the fall season started. Brigitte told me this as she sat on the windowsill leafing frantically through *Vogue* magazine while biting her nails.

The last time I'd seen this kind of frantic *Vogue*-reading was back in the sixties. I was a student taking a short subway ride on the Upper East Side line. This was before I'd followed my childhood instinct to avoid subway transportation on any line.

I noticed the beautiful-looking actress Paula Prentiss wearing a white faux-fur coat, and this desperate leafing-through pages was her reading technique, too. Her actor husband sat next to her and observed the situation with a look of knowing resignation. All I wanted to know was why such a couple would be riding the subway.

The other clothing on the shelves and hangers was prostitution-style—open midriffs with large metal rings holding top and bottom barely together: iridescent white trench coats with slits all around—back, front, and sides; and lots of tiny black knit dresses with strings holding them together on the sides.

I saw one sweater in the style I'd been searching for, in a useless size, extra-small—the price, six hundred and fifty dollars.

I left the store as fast as I could. A panic attack was starting, caused by what I'd seen. It wasn't easy rushing down a long flight of steps—an illegally steep, ancient stairway—a violation apparently disregarded by the town building inspectors. I had to hold on tight to the handrail as I fled the tawdry atmosphere and shocking price range.

When the name of the store's one designer came up later on in conversation with other people, the Brigitte girl heard me say it was a trampy style. She suddenly became alert and said, "I don't like to think what we carry is trampy."

"Who could wear it?" I said.

"Rock stars wear these things to the Grammys," she said.

"But this is Nantucket," I said.

Then I decided to give up. I was worn out explaining botanical remedies and the history of everything. I saw the future—myself old and resigned, worn down by the world changes, the way I'd seen people even older than those in my parents' generation grow weary and sigh, shake their heads, and refuse to explain anymore.

IN THE restaurant, I knew that the best seat was at the counter near the door. In that spot, the breeze came in, helped by a dust-filled window fan nearby. I went down to the other end of the counter where different animal parts were thrown onto the grill right in front of the eyes of the diners. A door was open behind that section of the counter and grill—open to the patio where John Kerry liked to sit when he was the candidate. But no one cared about that anymore.

People had become hopeless that they could change anything now that they no longer lived in a democracy, and they'd gone back to halfheartedly caring about their own little lives.

I didn't think about John Kerry much, either, after seeing him in a more upper-class restaurant, where, after he stood up to leave, he tied a cotton crew-neck sweater around his shoulders. Intentionally and falsely casual, copied year after year by Ralph L.— the tying of the sweater—how could John Kerry not have known better? Especially after having spent a day in his youth sailing with President—or at that time, Senator—John Kennedy?

I THOUGHT I'd stop and say hello to the fill-in hostess and her friend the Brigitte girl.

The hostess was an Italian-olive-lover. She'd told me that during her childhood in Rome in the nineteen-eighties, her mother would give her a hundred lire for a treat and she'd buy olives wrapped in brown paper shaped into a cone. No olives in this country tasted like those.

From this childhood came her natural abhorrence of hideous foods sold in supermarkets. This reminded me of the tiny Japanese helper who had questioned the bottle of Heinz white vinegar in the kitchen. It was used for cleaning, and the question was whether it was edible.

In front of these two young women, on the counter, were matching salads, the restaurant's most unhealthful one. "Only a man could think up such an unhealthy salad," a friend of mine liked to say about Caesar salads.

This one was a romaine lettuce cut in half lengthwise and covered with a thick white dressing. Instead of croutons, there were long slices of bread, all croutoned-up with garlic and olive oil or maybe even butter. The rumor around town was that Teresa Heinz Kerry had this dressing jetted off to her in Idaho during the winter. When this was repeated in front of the chef, he said, in defense of Teresa and her husband, *"Once* jetted there. Only because it's their favorite dressing."

There must have been an ingredient in the salad dressing that made people want to eat more and more of it. Maybe it contained one of those secret trans-fats or other bad fats that were added to foods to make them addictive. It wasn't exactly salt, it wasn't exactly sugar or oil, but a combination of the three whipped together to cause the desire for more. The chef had admitted that he didn't prepare his own mayonnaise but used a jar of it from his supplier. This was the answer.

I knew that the two women-girls would leave most of the dressing on their plates. I said, "Hello to you two who have both ordered the richest salad there is."

They glanced nonchalantly at their plates and said, "Sit down with us," but I knew they didn't mean it.

"I'm going to sit at the breezy end of the counter and order a bottle of water."

"No, you can't go to the front. Sit with us," the olive girl said.

"It's cooler there," I said. "And no sights of the grill."

They laughed that laugh Norma had for vegetarian themes.

"I forgot about that," the olive girl said. "She wants to be friends with Paul McCartney," she told Brigitte.

"But why? He dyes his hair."

"His children will fix that," I said. "He's the only vegetarian I know of to be friends with. And his whole family is in agreement." I pictured my husband's family of carnivores.

"I'm hoping to meet Stella McCartney for a job interview when I'm in London," Brigitte said.

"If you want to work with her, you'll have to convert," I said. "No animal foods, no animal clothes, no smoking."

A downcast expression appeared on her smooth-skinned face.

Olive was smiling.

The two young women continued eating their salad as they spoke. One thing I'd noticed before, when watching the Brigitte girl eat the salad, was that she never paused to use a napkin to blot the creamy dressing from her mouth.

The first time we dined together, a chance meeting at the counter, I was surprised to see an aspiring model eat such a highly caloric salad dressing. As we talked, I did notice, in fascination and then in distress, that the girl had this creamy white dressing at the corners of her mouth. I had put the sight out of my mind—even when she said about her jacket, "It's vintage," I didn't think about the white salad dressing. I had no reason to continue to have ill thoughts of her.

But here it was again, maybe three years later, and no one had given her any dining-etiquette tips. Her fiancé was the hip kind of guy these kinds of girls marry—a rock-concert-impresario, or one of those kinds of jobs—and even he hadn't taken a napkin and blotted the mouth of his beloved.

I'd seen a photo of him before—or what's called a photo nowadays—when she'd whisked out her cell phone, a tiny silver thing—before the RAZR phone had been invented—and flipped it open and showed me: "Look, here he is."

She was smiling. I could barely see on the tiny screen with the reflection of the light and the darkness of the background, but I did say, "Very cute. Very handsome." I would have said the same if she'd shown me a pumpkin head or a Halloween mask.

Soon the waiter came and removed the unfinished plates of salad. I'd been watching the sous-chef cook up the main course in a pan right behind the counter. What it was I didn't want to know. Although it did have some orange vegetables and light green other ingredients piled up together in an artistic mound.

The waiter put the plates down in front of the two friends.

"And what would you like?" the sous-chef asked me. "These vegetables?"

"What are they?" I asked. "The orange and the green."

"The orange is squash, the light green is actually spinach fettuccini. And then mushrooms—two kinds."

"That's spinach?" Olive said. "The Ebola spinach?"

"E. coli, not Ebola," Brigitte corrected her while laughing at the absurdity of the mistake.

"Oh, that's right, E. coli," Olive said, laughing too.

I knew Olive was one of those who either had a short attention span or pretended to, as a defense tactic or a low-grade, unconscious, passive-aggressive technique. I'd been a victim of this, spending a long time explaining facts about botanical remedies she could just as easily have found on Ask Dr. Weil.

She'd ask me, "What's that for again?" And I'd recently gone out of my way to buy her a box of raspberry-leaf tea after she'd spent an entire evening talking about the affliction of female-complaint cramps.

"I'm worn out explaining it," I said. "Look on Ask Dr. Weil."

"Huh? Is that his Web site?" she'd said.

I sympathized with tales of this painful disorder. "I thought new medications had put an end to all that," I'd said. "I recall a big improvement in the decades after Aleve and Motrin."

"No, no improvement," she'd said. "Why should there be these cramps?"

"Biology intended for us to be pregnant from age twelve to forty-four," I'd said.

"Oh no," Olive and Brigitte had said at the same time.

I'd read that overnourishment and dependence on animal foods—all that estrogen, especially the hormones injected into animals raised to grow faster to be killed for food for humans—this caused childbearing age to start earlier and earlier. It also caused boys and men to develop mammary glands in Argentina, where beef was king.

Then, birth control allowed the postponement or avoidance of pregnancy altogether. Estrogen production every month, year after year, wasn't what biology intended—all those ovulations wasted. That was the cause of cramps. Biology provided for pregnancies and nursing, a none-too-reliable form of birth control. In between, you're outside gathering berries and nuts. This keeps you fit and thin like a ballerina.

I'd learned about the subject from Dr. Arnold Loquesto, the world-renowned reproductive surgeon and endocrinologist: After having ten to twelve children, women died from complications of childbirth around age forty-four, and their husbands kept on reproducing with thirty-five- to forty-year-olds, women whose husbands had been killed by lions or snake bites. My imagination had filled in this last part.

Birth control and improved obstetrical care resulted in PMS, cramps, fibroids, and dependence on artificial forms of exercise.

I had summed this up for Olive and Brigitte. They didn't like it.

And there Olive was, asking that kind of question again. At least it wasn't directed only at me. Ebola indeed, I was thinking to myself, since there was no one there to whom I could speak the words.

I certainly was surprised that Brigitte knew the difference between Ebola and E. coli. She explained: "E. coli is the bacteria that gets in raw vegetables and food contaminated by farm animals. Ebola is the virus that they have in Africa. It kills you. Blood pours out of your head and you bleed to death," she said matter-of-factly.

"Oh, that's right. Now I remember," Olive said.

"E. coli attacks the digestive systems and all the organs shut down," Brigitte continued.

I sat back in astonishment. It wasn't easy to sit back on the counter seat without excellent spinal flexibility, and a coccyx injury from 1975 made the maneuver even more difficult.

"I didn't know you knew so much about these things," I said. I was impressed, to say the least. She had a future beyond fashion. I was happy for her.

"I don't like to dwell on them," she said. "I'm healthy. As a child I was on my own. My mother didn't have time to give us attention. She had to work. I ate food off the floor. I ate handfuls of raw meat and I never got sick once. I have good immune systems to all these things because I don't worry over them."

"Not Ebola and E. coli," the sous-chef said with a big smile. "Do you want mushrooms and basmati rice?" he asked me. "They're mixed, shiitakes and others," he said. I agreed to his offer.

"You know what I mean," Brigitte said, continuing to eat her dinner. "Children are likely to be more affected because they haven't built up their immunities."

"That little cute boy in the newspaper," Olive said. We all pictured the boy who'd died from the E. coli spinach. In the photo he was wearing a tiny bow tie.

"And then there's botulism," Brigitte said. Her knowledge had probably come from the botulism connection to the cosmetic-drug injections.

"I used to have a botulism phobia," I said. "After a canned mushroom killed several people in the nineteen-seventies."

I remembered the girl was too young to know this. Time was passing faster with every subject. "I read that one eighth of a canned mushroom tainted with botulinin toxin can kill hundreds," I said.

"Really? How? When was it?" Olive asked.

"Around 1972. Canned vichyssoise killed a man. His wife was saved. The doctors figured it out too late for his treatment—the antitoxin."

"I thought it was from turkey," Olive said.

"That's salmonella," the sous-chef said.

"I thought people died from turkey when I was in high school," Olive said.

"Botulism can grow only in a vacuum," the sous-chef said. "Anaerobic."

I knew the two girl-women were familiar with the word "aerobic" from their interest in fitness, but "anaerobic" would be news to them.

"I have to go outside to make a call," Brigitte said. "My friend stopped his schizophrenia medication and got sent to the hospital just because he was telling someone about a radio-wave invention that could go through his head. He's very brilliant and it happens to be a factual invention."

She took out her phone, a black RAZR this time.

"Why did you get black?" I asked.

"It's a RAZR," she said with condescension and disbelief.

"Mine is silver," I said. "I thought you'd have silver, too."

I took it out of my canvas book bag. This placated her and she got up. She'd explain about the color later, I guessed. The year before, she was glad to hear that we both had silver Apple PowerBooks, or titanium, as she liked to say. I didn't tell her I used mine only for the weather reports and to order vitamins— this was before the Paul McCartney Google Alert had become available. She used hers for everything.

"I didn't know she was so well informed," I said to Olive after Brigitte had gone outside.

"Oh, she's very smart. And her boyfriend is, too. They're not only good-looking, they're both really nice."

"These mushrooms look canned," I said to the sous-chef when the small bowl arrived.

"Only the black ones are. I'll do them over—just shiitakes."

Why go to restaurants anyway, I was thinking as usual. For the entertainment, for the "All the World's a Stage" element.

"Do you boil the mushrooms before you sauté them?" I asked him. "Just in case?"

"If we see a weird can we don't use it. We notify someone immediately."

Brigitte had returned in time to hear this.

"Are you still on botulism?" she asked. She was amused.

"I didn't suspect them of using canned mushrooms," I said.

"I should go home before the cramps start again," Olive said.

"Did you take Aleve?" I asked her.

"I took Motrin yesterday, but it didn't work. Someone gave

me a Percocet and I took half and I started to get a weird feeling in my head."

"Percocet is bad," I said. "Take half a Vicodin."

"Can you take that with Motrin and Percocet?" she asked. "I'm afraid of all these drugs. Me and Jayne were talking to the pharmacist about it."

"'Jayne and I,'" I said.

"But last week you told me it was 'Jayne and me.'"

"I said, 'Objective—gave some Percocet to Jayne and me.' 'Jayne and I are going to the pharmacy'—SUBJECTS."

That Miss Jean Brodie feeling was starting to creep in.

"You know I lived in Italy until eighth grade," Olive said. "I missed all that."

"Now you're forty-two," I said. I was getting that feeling in my head, too. Not a Percocet head, but the head that comes from explaining this rule of grammar.

"I once took Motrin and Aleve and codeine, and it didn't help," Brigitte said.

"Start with cramp bark in raspberry-leaf tea a week before," I said. "Work up to the hard stuff."

"What's the cramp bark again?" Olive asked.

I knew where we were heading.

"Someone recommended that at the health-food store, but I was afraid to take it," she said. "Will I wake up at four a.m. with cramps? Then I can't take anything else for eight hours after Aleve."

"Take Aleve at midnight," Brigitte said, showing a bit of annoyance.

"When I was a teenager, I begged my mother for a razor," Olive told us. "I said, 'I'm going to slit my wrists.'"

"When I was twelve, I begged for a hysterectomy," I said. "My mother wouldn't allow us any medications. Once, one of my older sisters took eight aspirin."

"At the same time?" Olive asked.

"Within a few hours. She said she didn't care if she died," I said. "Those were the dark ages of cramps."

"I heard they'd say, 'It's psychological,'" Olive said. She started to laugh.

"Our mothers were primitive and unenlightened. Doctors, too."

"This one time, I was at the beach when the cramps started," Brigitte said. "I ran to my car and my fiancé drove me to the Stop & Shop to get some Advil. On the way, it got so bad I took three Motrin from the glove compartment."

"They must have been hot in there."

"Can you take that together?" Olive asked.

"They're ibuprofen; they're the *same thing*," I said.

"Well anyway, I didn't know what I was doing," Brigitte said. "He ran in and got me the Advil and I took three more. When I got home I took two more. Suddenly I got really hot all over and broke out into a cold sweat. I felt I was going faint."

"See? That's what I'm afraid of," Olive said.

"All that and still no relief from the cramps! I couldn't believe it!"

I thought back to the time I'd first seen her with her face

puffy. It could have been the night after the ordeal she'd just described. I felt guilt and remorse for my thoughts.

The conversation continued without the two friends making much headway toward understanding a cure. After a while, I was barely listening and gave up saying anything. Then I got an idea. The kind of idea where lightbulbs are drawn in comic books to show a bright idea. But this bulb wasn't bright with little sparkle lines around it. It was dull and without the sparkles.

"You both have fibroids," I announced. "I can tell from the symptoms."

"Really? Everything we always talk about?" Olive said.

"Yes," I said. "Exactly. You should go see the world-renowned reproductive surgeon Dr. Arnold Loquesto. He's an expert in a minor procedure to remove fibroids. You can go home the same day."

"I can't afford a sonogram," Brigitte said. "When I get to England I'll be in the NHS and it will be free."

During my last conversation with Dr. Loquesto, I'd asked him about the laser, roller-ball fibroid surgery that I'd read about in the *Times*. The patient was the woman Secretary of State, though at the time she was still National Security Adviser.

He'd said, "It's not that effective. It just reduces the size. It's very painful, postoperative."

"Don't they give morphine?" I'd asked.

"Yes, but morphine doesn't cover it."

I asked how that could be, and he said, "It just doesn't. It's that kind of pain."

I pictured the National Security Adviser in postoperative pain. Although she had participated in war crimes, lying, and warmongering, I didn't wish morphine-resistant pain on her.

Maybe the medical condition had caused her to look angry and unhappy so much of the time, smiling only when she was enthusiastically telling lies in front of the terror-attack-investigation commission.

Perhaps this pain had affected her decision-making powers, resulting in the first war started by an Alfred E. Neuman president, an evil vice president, and a woman with excruciatingly severe cramps. In the past, they did say that a woman shouldn't be president because of hormonal fluctuations making women emotional and unstable. They don't dare say it anymore, after the current male person in office.

I noticed Brigitte's profile. She was biting her nails on her left hand and untangling a knot in her hair with her right hand. The untangling went on and on.

"I've always been unlucky in love" was what I heard her saying to Olive. Before I could stupidly wonder how such a creature could be unlucky in love, I saw how sad she was underneath her newfound romantic happiness, with the unique, designed-by-her-fiancé diamond ring, and some designer dress; there was such a deep sadness I thought she might start to cry.

I guessed her childhood of lack of attention and eating food off the floor had left her unattended and neglected in other ways, too.

I recalled during my youth, at age nineteen, when an elderly

Hungarian dermatologist questioned some antianxiety medicine that had been prescribed for my condition. He'd said, "How could a healthy and lovely young woman have any problems?"

FINALLY WE left the diner. Olive and I were walking to our automobiles, which we shouldn't have driven to town. We'd both had reasons. Olive lived out of town. I'd left my car there earlier in the afternoon when it was still too hot to walk in. My plan had been to get to the flower store to look at some peach-colored nerines. I'd read in two of Dr. Weil's books that flowers were an important part of health. And I'd heard him say nerines were beautiful.

We'd walked a couple of blocks when Olive told Brigitte to be careful or she'd ruin her shoes—white ballet slipper–shoes. Brigitte named the designer. I'd had much better Capezio ballet slipper–shoes during my preteen years. One pair was lavender, with little bunches of pastel-colored straw instead of bows in front.

When my mother saw those Capezio ballet slipper–shoes in a window, she had to buy them, no matter the cost—seventeen dollars, at that time. I decided not to mention this and kept walking. What would these two care about my childhood shoes?

Brigitte lit a cigarette and quickly apologized.

"It's your face and your teeth, not just your health," I said, hoping this would influence her.

"I know," she said as she exhaled and tried to step around the puddles in her white slipper-shoes.

We walked her to her little clapboard house. She and Olive were still talking about cramp medications.

"I'll phone that surgeon for you," I called, as Brigitte went up the wooden steps.

After 11:00 p.m., it was too loud a call for the neighbors. But they were accustomed to drunken revelry from the summer students, and this sentence was less raucous.

As Olive and I walked to her car, she said she felt sick again.

"Take half a Vicodin right now," I said.

"Where to get it prescribed in this town is the question. They think everyone's an addict."

"But Vicodin doesn't make you feel good," I said.

"People like it," she said.

"I have eleven left over from a dental procedure," I said. "You can have some."

We devised a plan. She'd drive me to my car and follow me home. I'd give her the pills.

OLIVE SAID she liked the kitchen.

"Too bad you don't own this house," she said. "The kitchen is big and light, but not all done up."

"Our kitchen at home is a third the size," I said. "I like to stay in this room most of the time. It's the only air-conditioned room downstairs."

"You could have dinner parties in the little dining room in the winter with the fireplace going. Wouldn't that be fun? If you had five million dollars."

I pictured the scene. People gave dinners all winter, when the restaurants closed. They kept each other entertained—like performers, not like Martha Stewart's depictions of people at dinners. Each person was a stand-up act—comedy and tragedy or monologues about the absurdity of their lives on the island in winter.

I showed Olive my large vitamin collection on the counter and then the small pharmaceutical part.

"Here are the Vicodin and Aleve," I said.

I poured a few Aleve and two Vicodin into one bottle.

"Great. But will I wake up at four a.m. if I take it now?"

"Oh no, not that question," I said. "Did you look on Ask Dr. Weil?"

"What's that again? A Web site?"

I'd brought a few copies of his books, but I was always giving them away. I had that PowerBook, but it was often acting up, with the many-colored spinning ball causing trouble.

"I better go home to sleep," Olive said. "I have to open the bookstore early. The manager wants to be first on line at the thrift-shop sale to get a fondue pot he's been looking at all year. Can you believe that?"

"I heard that this happens to people who stay here all winter."

"That's why I want to get off this island so badly," she said.

"Why would he want a fondue pot?" I asked. Even when first

invented they were too ugly. They were jokes about the worst wedding presents.

He'd come to that fireplace dinner bringing a contribution, and we'd all see the pot of fondue he'd prepared. That was the life in the winter. I couldn't help imagining a red Dansk fondue pot from the nineteen-seventies—even worse, the hideous black fondue forks, to say nothing of the fat-saturated and oil-coated fondue.

Half the people I knew wanted to live on Nantucket all year, but couldn't figure out how. The other half wanted to leave and they didn't know how. Then there were the lucky few who lived there and left for January and February. It was possible to have all one's conversations on this topic.

At last, Olive went home to keep thinking about the various medications.

I wanted to watch David Letterman and I decided to look on Ask Dr. Weil at the same time. Then I'd print out the information and fax it to the bookstore for her.

I was wondering why I didn't know anyone else to talk to.

T HE NEXT night I was trying to get to the bookstore again. I was hoping the vegan hostess would be back so Olive could have some time off from one of her jobs, but as I passed by the restaurant, I saw that she was outside talking to some diners who were waiting for their tables.

We waved hello and she told me that things were under control. At least she didn't say, "Cool."

"The manager decided he didn't want the fondue pot after all and he went in early and opened the store."

I was relieved. I didn't like to think of him waiting on line for the pot.

"Did you read the faxes I sent you from Ask Dr. Weil?"

"Where'd you send them? Here?"

"No, to the bookstore."

"Oh, right. I forgot all about that. I saw them, but I'm like, Oh, I'll read them later. The Vicodin really worked, by the way. Thanks!"

"But before you know it, weeks will pass. You want to be prepared."

"That tea, what is it again?"

"Don't you have the box?"

"Well, I guess I do. I haven't tried it."

"You know, I bought you some cramp bark tincture but I'm not giving it to you unless you'll try it." The raspberry-leaf tea cost less than the cramp-bark tincture.

"What's that for again?"

I imagined how Dr. Weil himself must feel. He was more patient than I was. His years of meditation and breathing and gardening and swimming and yoga had paid off. And then the invention of Ask Dr. Weil. That alone justified the technology of the hideous word "Internet."

But what about those who wouldn't ask Dr. Weil? First, the years of Olive's working in the bookstore and the sentence, "Do we even have his book? Wait, I'll look."

I thought about all the time I'd spent waiting for that one book to be found.

"Oh, I was looking for *Health and Healing*," she'd said for a few years.

"But that's a medical history—not a remedy book," I'd say.

"Why would a publisher give two books almost the same titles?" she'd say.

"That's a good point," I said.

"I BETTER go in," Olive said. "Will you come back after the bookstore? You can have some Panna water."

I looked into the diner. The sous-chef was throwing those animal parts onto the grill. The main chef was pouring sauce into the sauté pan. Later on, they'd be scrubbing everything with steel wool, but no amount of scouring could erase what went on there. I'd read that an Orthodox Jewish dietary law provided—as a method of purification—not only sand-blasting stoves but burying defiled cooking utensils in the earth or sand for a certain number of days. Earth and sand were everywhere all around us on Nantucket.

I was wondering about Paul McCartney being voted the most popular vegetarian in England. Would he sit at the counter with the sight of the grill in front of his eyes? Did he restrict his dining out to only vegetarian restaurants the way Orthodox Jews and Muslims did? Since I didn't know him, there was no way to tell. I didn't know anyone to ask. I didn't know anyone at all.

HAPPY TRAILS TO YOU

PEOPLE SAY "GOOD MORNING," but don't believe them. It's just something to say. I don't recall "Good morning" being said during my childhood, except in kindergarten. "Good morning, Miss Murphy," we all had to say, but we didn't mean it. We lived in fear.

We didn't even know what it meant. I had a general idea and naturally went along with the "Good morning." The Pledge of Allegiance was the next part of the routine I didn't understand, but I went right along with that, too, thinking as many children did that "pledgeofallegiance" was one word.

A scary part was "for which it stands." I understood the word to be "Witchitstans," a republic of witches in control of America—just the way it is now. Later on in life, I remembered my father laughing when I gave my explanation of the Pledge of Allegiance. He laughed hard and with a kind of joy that made his large blue eyes look even larger and brighter and gave him an elflike resemblance to the Duke of Windsor. He was taller than the Duke and more intelligent, too.

In a documentary I'd seen about the Duke—then Prince of Wales—he was shown in old film footage traveling all over the world. The narrator said that at this time, 1935—when the Duke was still Prince Edward—he "was the most popular man in the world." Throngs came out to greet him, just as they did later on for President Kennedy and Elvis Presley.

I hadn't heard of the Duke at age five, but one of my older sisters, filled with erudition from a very early age, pointed out the resemblance when she was only fourteen. She told me the whole story, which I found as fascinating as she did. She said that the Duke of Windsor had the saddest look in his large blue eyes because of his dreadful mistake of abdication and then being sent off to do nothing in Bermuda and other places all over the world. We felt sorry for the Duke. His Nazi-sympathizing and personal acquaintance with Hitler was still kept secret from the world at that time, or didn't receive much attention compared to the amount given to his weird marriage choice and his life which followed.

One reason that my sister knew so many facts and spouted them constantly in expressionless sentences was that she was alone in her room so much with that *Encyclopaedia Britannica Junior*. She was always reading and keeping facts in her head, never playing with other children or seeming to have much fun. Her inability to get over my having been born was the problem.

"You were the most beautiful baby ever born" was said over and over by neighbors and family and friends, although I never took this in, thinking it was something said to all children. The comparison to my sister's own spooky countenance—this might have been what set her up for a life of gathering information.

Many years later, I felt sorry about all this. My parents' method of dealing with the situation—failing to consult any of the German-refugee psychiatric experts who were in abundance in the United States after the war—must have allowed the damage to become permanent. Instead of seeking any advice, their method was to keep secret any good qualities I might have had. One of those clever German psychoanalysts told me something startling—too late to help—when I was thirty-five. Since her specialty was child development, she said she'd "seen one child completely destroyed to protect the other." I didn't take this seriously at the time.

Why didn't our backward, screwed-up mother bring us to this child development expert at the time the tragedy was in progress? It was too much for her—she can't be blamed. She had her own sad upbringing. When I was eight, she gave me her childhood ring, a gold ring with her initials engraved onto the oval center. She told me a story about how she had begged her own mother for a ring at the same age and had finally gotten this one.

Before that, she said, she used to sit on the steps in front of their house and make herself a ring with a peach pit for a stone. This was too heartbreaking for me to ask any more questions. I wondered about it, too, because peach pits are big. But this must have been in the era when peaches were normal-sized—before they had been jazzed up with growth hormones and chemical fertilizers. I tried to picture the smallest peach pit I could, but still thought a smooth-looking apricot pit would have been better and more the right size and color. My sister had informed me that apricot pits contained cyanide and you would die if you swallowed one. But the raised edge around apricot pits would have been decorative, for a realistic ring-stone appearance.

What did I do then? I tried on the ring—it had no stone. Maybe I went to my room and cried for my mother and her peach-pit ring. I did a lot of crying in my childhood—not as much as later on, as an attempted grown-up. I wore the ring but couldn't look at the oval initialed part without thinking of my mother on those steps, and of her mother, probably in the kitchen peeling potatoes. Not that potato peeling is so bad—it's not like the step scrubbing of Dorothy McGuire, the mother in *A Tree Grows in Brooklyn*. There's even a video of Paul McCartney peeling potatoes to prepare mashed potatoes. He peels incorrectly, with a paring knife, toward his valuable, important thumb.

Another ring I owned did have a stone—the ring came in a Cracker Jack box and the stone was a dark-green-glass oval with the letter "A" on it. The goal was to find a ring with your own initial.

"'A' for assassinate," my sister said when she saw the ring.

This was her idea of fun because a murder had taken place in an apartment building around the corner from our house the day before. My mother tried to keep this from us while my sister tried to rev it up, saying, "'A' for assassinate" as many times as she could.

That was a ring I never wore, but, on the bright side, I did learn the long "A" word, "assassinate," at age five or six, a word that didn't come back up until 1963, and forever after a word and event always on my mind.

I didn't think we had such things as assassinations in our wonderful, perfect country of good mornings, the Pledge of Allegiance, and the daily bread I imagined to be Bond white or Wonder Bread when we were forced to recite the Lord's prayer in sixth grade.

There was a Memorial Day special event on the school stage the same year, and we had to memorize the poem "In Flanders Fields." We had no idea why. I still have it memorized. But now I know what it means.

We also had to memorize Rudyard Kipling's poem "If." I didn't really feel connected to it because of the last line, " . . . you'll be a Man, my son!" I must have been an unconscious feminist at that young age.

There was a rumor that our elderly teacher, Miss Hickman, had lost her fiancé in World War I. Perhaps she'd forgotten that World War II had occurred more recently. I had seen photographs of those crosses but couldn't take the meaning into my eleven-year-old mind. Tragedy on a grand scale was new to all in sixth grade. I was also distracted by the grammar of "between the crosses row on row," when I thought it should have been "among the crosses."

Then, as we all know, after World War I a number of dreadful events continued to occur—and then more, from 1963 up through the horrible new century.

I DIDN'T recall anyone saying "Good morning" when I lived in New York or Boston or any city. But I might have been partly to blame because when I lived in cities I dreaded going out into them, and by the time I got outside, it was afternoon.

When I moved to the country the only person who said "Good morning" was the Polish landscape-maintenance man and his helper. I had to go outside to talk to him every week to decide what work needed to be done. Then there was the same greeting from his assistant, the rosy-cheeked young Polish woman, who must have learned the phrase as part of learning English, unaware of how rude people are in America, and how obsolete and unfashionable the greeting. It was always a surprise to hear it—a pleasant surprise, even though I knew they didn't mean it.

In Nantucket, on the best part of the island, the privileged, wealthy residents could be seen walking outside, saying "Good morning" to each other. They used each other's names, too. "Good morning, Bill," "Good morning, Jim," could be heard on every lane.

★   ★   ★

AFTER AGE forty, I started thinking about my parents and my childhood home. I wished they'd never sold their big old house with fireplaces in the living and dining rooms, and fruit trees in the garden. I missed my parents and my aunts and uncles, especially my favorite aunt, who worked in a toy company. Sometimes, when she saw me, she would start to sing, "Did you ever see a dream walking? That's you." I didn't take that to mean anything about myself, either, but I loved the way she looked when she sang it. Also, I was distracted by trying to imagine what a dream walking would be.

Now in the terrible 2000s I didn't have one person, especially one vegetarian person, I could talk to. I didn't know any vegetarians, especially not Paul McCartney. He would have been perfect!

All my close relatives were gone, except that sister—the middle sister had moved to Tibet. As might be expected, I hadn't spoken to the first one since she disregarded my father's condition of old age and did nothing to prevent his decline. The Duke of Windsor, at least, received excellent medical care with every comfort and dignity.

My mental state didn't lead to the right frame of mind for socializing. Most of my friends and acquaintances had similar dramas going on at the same time I did. There were younger people, but the ones I knew were empty-headed and liked to smoke. They loved to smoke. They could have a ten-minute so-called conversation about how much they loved the deadly addiction. Others ate dead animals. One liked to order that dish "pulled pork"—I didn't want to know what it was—and I had to sit at the other end of the counter when she ordered this. "A little baby pig," I said to her, to no effect. Others in this group ate animals *and* smoked.

Paul McCartney was not in my social circle. I had no circle. Why couldn't he and I have tea together? Just as friends. Maybe he'd sing a song in the middle of the teatime, or get an idea for a song or a melody, or even a few words. Maybe he'd hum a tune or play his mandolin. No. It didn't happen. And I knew of not one other vegetarian with whom to talk or have tea, even without the singing and the mandolin.

THEN CAME the dreaded phone call. All phone calls are to be dreaded. That must have been what Dorothy Parker meant by saying, when the phone rang, "What fresh hell is this?" To think I didn't know what she meant when I first read that quote. At the time, there were still some good phone calls in my life. Also, the word "fresh" didn't seem quite right to describe any kind of hell.

This new phone call was one of those where an agent, trying to sound enthusiastic, reports a request for an interview.

"Oh no, please, not that," I kept myself from saying. The interviewer was a big fan and had tracked the agent down.

After a few terrorizing minutes of discussion, we decided

that the interviewer would submit written questions. He was so desperate he'd agree to anything. His typed note of request was beseechingly desperate and polite, with a tiny spark of confidence. "I'm a good phone person" was the spark.

I thought I knew what he meant. I myself am just like Marilyn Monroe in the phone preference department—as well as a few other departments. I would rather talk on the phone than have to come face-to-face with another human being. Face-to-face—or is it eyes-to-eyes?

One thing I didn't have was that big, beautiful white phone Marilyn Monroe had. But there was one thing I did have that she didn't have—caller ID.

After the interviewer and I finally spoke a few times, he said, "You must be a Luddite." I agreed. Then he asked, since he was twenty-nine, if there were any inventions of modern technology I liked. All I could think of was caller ID, the best invention of modern times. Before that, first place was held by Tampax. Penicillin was old hat. I didn't mention those.

I never answered the phone unless I knew who it was, and was learning never to answer, no matter who it was. Even what passes for a "ring" now gives me a fit of anxiety, or that tight, clenched-up feeling in the chest area, probably the precursor to a future heart attack. What happened to the original, one kind of telephone ring of yesteryear? If Dorothy Parker had had the good fortune brought by caller ID, at least she would have known what kind of hell to expect.

I'd started my phone preference when I began thinking

about the difficulty of faces, sometime in the nineteen-eighties. It began with this thought or feeling: What is a person? Is a person a face? Eyes, behind the eyes? What is the meaning of a face? Where should we look when we speak to a person—at the eyes? Into the eyes? At how the eyes are working with the eyebrows? The furrows between the brows and the way they work along with the eyes?

Should we look at the place where the words are coming from? What if we spot some dental work of a distracting nature? Something gold. Or a silver wire. Or teeth with such big fillings that they have a bluish-grey cast.

Then there's the skin on the face—perhaps rosy cheeks and a small precise nose. Eyelashes without mascara and soft wispy eyebrows. Thin, wispy, light-brown hair. What does it all add up to—a face? A man's short hair going every which way with some grey all through it. Brown eyes, then a nose, thin, but hooking down too much. What is this person, what he is saying or how his face looks? What is the meaning of his churlish hair?

Swept away by the meaninglessness of people's faces, I gradually lost the ability to talk to them. "What is a face?" would come into my mind every time I looked at one. But I'd continue the conversation and no one would be the wiser.

How do people understand each other's faces? They take them for granted. Not like me—stunned and bewildered, each time one appeared in front of me. Just the thought of having to face a new face was enough to make me shudder with fright.

I saw a number of psychiatrists and psychoanalysts during this time—not because of this one problem—they actually added to the problem. Because every one of these psychiatrists' faces had something really wrong with it.

WHEN I received the interviewer's questions, I prepared myself. I knew the hell of those questions. But when I read the first ones, I flew into a rage.

I had diagnosed a minor manic-depressive state for myself many years before. I asked a British psychiatrist about it—I was trying to help him along since he had no ideas of his own— "Aren't I a manic-depressive? At least, a minor manic-depressive?" He just laughed and said, "Maybe a little bit."

Since his analysis was obviously a failure—he was always busy with his own thoughts and connections and stream of consciousness—he must have been thinking that the use of the word "minor" was amusing—he was accustomed to the word used for "minor poet" or "minor artist." He must have heard it used only in this context. Naturally, he wouldn't address the matter in any helpful way, so the mental condition continued and even worsened. The British—too repressed to speak the truth, too embarrassed, too polite, too eccentric, too aristo-cratic—everything to disqualify and bar them from the profes-sion, if it can be called a profession.

My favorite writer, Thomas Bernhard, had written in my favorite of his books, *Wittgenstein's Nephew:* "Of all medical practitioners, psychiatrists are the most incompetent. All my life I have dreaded nothing so much as falling into the hands of psychiatrists, beside whom all other doctors, disastrous though they may be, are far less dangerous, for in our present-day society, psychiatrists are a law unto themselves and enjoy total immunity, and after studying the methods they practiced quite unscrupulously . . . for so many years, my fear became yet more intense. Psychiatrists are the real demons of our age, going about their business with impunity and constrained by neither law nor conscience."

This quote often popped into my mind. Real demons was the part I liked best.

THE FIRST question on the boy interviewer's list was "Why is it so difficult to reach you? Most artists and photographers have"—he dared to say that terrible un-word—"a Web site, or they teach at universities."

My first impulse was to crumple up the paper, or, controlling that impulse, to write on the page, "That's what agents are for." The only pen I had handy was a red-ink pen and after I'd madly scribbled answers to the questions I decided it was all a waste of time. I left the paper around here and there until I discovered it a couple of weeks later and thought it looked so ugly—the red scribbles—that I tore it up and threw it away. I was too disgusted to walk to the shredder-fax-printer room.

I'd read that Edna St. Vincent Millay expressed a desire to

slap the face of an interviewer who asked a question she found especially stupid.

I finally agreed to a preliminary talk with the eager interviewer. After we spoke, I began to feel sorry for him. This was when I started to think of him as Interviewer Boy. His questions about MFA photography programs being worthwhile—I had always found those questions somewhat pathetic—the part about believing one could be taught a talent to do anything. Students believed this in their earnest way.

It turned out that the misguided boy interviewer *was* good on the phone. He was like a fun friend—always in a cheerful mood, unlike my friends, who had all begun to be beaten down by life. When I told him that, he laughed his head off—this mood of cheer, even though he lived on the very worst kind of junk food and, even more terrible, cigarettes. He lived in the one hipster part I knew of in Texas, a part where people were still polite. He said, "I hope you don't mind if I'm eating my lunch. It's a ham-and-cheese-and-potato-chip sandwich on white bread." I minded the contents, not that he was dining while speaking. I said so, too. Maybe I said, "Oh no," or "Oh God, not that."

"Couldn't you at least buy some Ezekiel bread?" I asked. "It's all sprouted grains."

"Ezekiel bread," he said. "My father asks me to bring him a carful of that from Whole Foods every time I go up to visit them. They don't have it there."

"Here," I said. "Listen to the label: 'As described in the Holy

Scriptures, "Take also unto thee *Wheat* and *Barley* and *Beans* and *Lentils* and *Millet* and *Spelt* and put them in one vessel and make bread of it . . ." *Ezekiel 4:9.'"

"This is like talking to my father."

"You mean the biblical verse part?"

"Yeah. That's a conversation with him."

THE INTERVIEWER'S beverages for starting the morning were two cans of Mountain Dew, something I'd heard of but had never seen in person. I could take a guess what the ingredients were. But to wake up to cans of that for the "Good morning" I'd learned about at an early age? Whatever it was—that drink—and cigarettes—how could we converse and prepare for the interview?

He lived two blocks from Whole Foods, but he never had any whole foods, or any food, in his refrigerator or kitchen cabinets. He'd say, "I'm so hungry. I just ran five miles."

He'd walk to his refrigerator, phone in hand, and say, "Hmmm, let's see—maraschino cherries—I think I'll have those for lunch. They're my favorite."

Sometimes he'd find a bottle of olives in there, but they were the old-fashioned green ones, stuffed with dyed pimentos. If he was hungry between meals of those cherries and stuffed olives, he'd say, "I have to have a Little Debbie." I'd never heard about those cakes except as a joke on David Letterman's show or somewhere.

I quickly researched Little Debbie. Although I hate computers, even the wireless silver Apple I owned for emergencies, I found the information. It was from the *Vegetarian Journal*. A reporter had inquired and been told that the Glazed Cake Donut did not contain animal by-products. Even the mono- and diglycerides were from non-animal sources. Little Debbie's distributor was owned by a Seventh-Day Adventist family. "However," the reporter said, "they gave no indication that this belief system is the reason that the donut does not contain animal products."

I found this fascinating since none of the other ingredients were healthful—cornstarch, sugar, the usual.

THE INTERVIEWER often seemed surprised to find his refrigerator empty even though he rarely bought any food. It was as if he expected food to magically appear in there.

"Can't you just buy some fruit?" I asked. "Fruit and vegetables?"

"I suppose I could. But one time I bought fruit and it went bad before I could eat it."

It wasn't until months had gone by that I discovered he didn't keep fruit in the refrigerator. He left it out in a big bowl.

"Put the whole bowl in the refrigerator," I said. "That's easy."

"Are you supposed to?" he asked. "I never knew that."

Most food-preparation activities were "too hard" or "too

much trouble," he usually said. "Olive oil and vinegar? I'm not good at mixing things," he'd said once.

The next time we spoke, he said he'd dined on jars of cherries and olives, potato chips, Snickers, and Little Debbies.

"Do you know what food is?" I asked.

"I guess I know, but I choose to disregard it. I should get a glucose test."

"Couldn't you eat a peach? They have all those organically grown white peaches at Whole Foods."

"Do you know how huge these markets are? To walk around after running five or nine miles?"

"You could drink fruit juice from real fruit."

Every time I named a fruit he'd say, "I love those!" But he couldn't manage to buy anything that wasn't made in a factory and sealed in a box, can, or plastic wrapper. I told him about Amy's organic frozen dinners, but he said he was afraid they might be too healthful.

"The secretary in my office is a vegan, and now she's on to Amy's vegan frozen burritos," he said. "She's the one who criticized me: 'Every day you eat a Snickers bar.'"

"Does the secretary know the rest?"

"She couldn't imagine. Only my friends know. You're the only one who hasn't given up on me."

"You could be a case study. Present yourself to Dr. Andrew Weil."

"There's that movie, *Super Size Me,* about McDonald's. Isn't it great?"

"It's okay, but the filmmaker didn't have to eat there three times a day. Dr. Weil is science. You would be an extreme case. Do you ever eat a vegetable?"

"Here, this is a vegetable—pickled okra. It's in the cabinet," he said.

"How about fresh okra? Kale and okra."

"How would I cook it? Isn't it complicated?"

A normal breakfast for him was Frosted Flakes, or Cheerios if lots of sugar was added, then a can of Mountain Dew. Once, when he was in college, a nutritionist asked the students to fill out a form on the subject of daily meals. On some forms, she wrote "More vegetables" or "More grains," "Less animal protein," "Less sugar." But on his form she simply wrote "This is terrible!" He thought it was funny and even seemed proud of his grade.

Other meals were Cheetos, Kraft Singles slices, Reese's peanut butter cups, Kit Kat bars, Twix, and a box of Chips Ahoy cookies. Sometimes he'd call from his truck while he was ordering lunch from a fast-food joint. I'd hear him say, "A number seven, Cheesy Potatoes, and a Coke." He had to explain to me what the potatoes were. If only I didn't have to know.

HE'D NEVER heard of the Duke of Windsor. I soon discovered this and the many other subjects about which he hadn't heard. At first I informed him about a few of these subjects but after a while I became exhausted and started saying, "Google it."

I knew from his age that he was tied to a computer and would always Google anything right on the spot. He'd never heard of Busby Berkeley, even though it was soon clear that the interviewer wasn't a heterosexual. I always know. I know before they know. When he mentioned the fact, I said, "Well, I assumed," and he said, "How? I never mentioned Judy Garland." Then he laughed in his good-natured way. I told him how: (1) his dog, a papillon; (2) his never mentioning a girlfriend; (3) the way he was so neat and organized; (4) his close relationship with his aunt, a famous interior designer in her fifties—how they talked on and off all day, how he described in detail a kind of lamp or chair she liked, and more.

There was a time when I realized that among those who said they liked my photographs there was a high percentage of gay guys. I once asked the photo editor of one of my books, "Is this going to be a Judy Garland thing?" He laughed and said no. I told this to the interviewer.

"Why? Do you have a problem with gay people?" the interviewer asked.

"The problem is discrimination against them. I was just wondering about the Judy Garland aspect back then."

Since first grade, I had sympathized and was friendly with sensitive boys who were teased by the other children—that sympathy and their attention to detail created our bond.

During any lull in the interview-conversation when we paused to think, Interviewer Boy would hum a happy tune. Although one bad thing did happen early on. A few days went by

and we hadn't spoken. We had postponed the interview because he had a long time before his deadline. We had gotten
into an endless phone conversation, the kind he had with his
aunt. I was worried that the interval was caused by some incident from his newly gay situation.

One odd thing about him and his gayness was that he wasn't
interested in flowers. I had formed several gay-guy acquain-
tanceships on the basis of flower-talk alone. He didn't know
what any plant, flower, or tree was, but he did know what a
pecan tree was, and I didn't even know that pecans grew on
trees. He pronounced the word "pecahn," and I kept to my
childhood pronunciation, "pécan."

My older sister was the first child in our neighborhood to
like butter pecan ice cream—a new flavor at the time. We lived
in the decades of the three basic flavors. After that, we were the
only two children who liked coffee ice cream. We liked orange
Life Savers and grape ice pops, while other children liked cherry
or lime. We liked the color lavender while others liked red. We
had that in common, and we knew we were different from the
masses. Saying "pécan" that old way reminded me of that one
good thing about my sister, though I regretted our having been
exposed to dairy products of any kind.

IN HIS childhood, the interviewer boy had sat under "pecahn"
trees with his grandfather, who called northerners "Yankees!"
He disliked Yankees and blamed things on them. The boy and

his grandfather would crack two pecan shells together with their hands and eat the pecans. That was all he knew about trees. I asked why his grandfather disliked northerners, and he said, "Oh, they're rude—brash, pretentious, snobby, and only care about money." I was surprised. I thought the whole country was like that. The money part, anyway.

An example of southern manners was to say, "May I place you on hold a moment?" instead of "I have to get this!" *Click.* He meant it. He'd always come right back apologizing.

I didn't know there were still good manners in the South. As for Texas, I knew of that one person in the White House and his evil Gang of Four. And, on that subject, I often thought, Cheney did not just "shoot an old man in the face," as Jon Stewart liked to say on *The Daily Show*. The many news reports stated these facts: he'd shot the man in the face *and* in the heart. The words "elderly man" would have been better, too. The pellets remained in the elderly man's heart, ready to start something medically serious going at any time. The pellets couldn't be removed. That was the worst part. It was never spoken about again.

WHENEVER I said I had to get off the phone to go out to search for plants—annuals, perennials, or shrubs—the interviewer couldn't understand why. He didn't know that there were only three important months for the gardening season—search in April, purchase and plant in May, complete in June, maintain in hot July and August—because in Texas it was always hot. He didn't know what spring was. He didn't know the planting season was short, and he couldn't understand the rush to three nurseries every day.

He was like Michael Caine when the actor was living in L.A. and bought a shrub rose at a nursery. I'd heard him talking on TV about asking, as Yankees and the British have to, "When can I plant it?" The answer was "When you get home," an amusing surprise to the actor, who was accustomed to the more northern climes of England.

The interviewer boy said most people didn't know about his gayness. He wasn't identifiably one of them. He didn't like that kind—he couldn't stand it. It was a new thing for him—one year, maybe, of facing it, years of unhappiness before. I wasn't really listening since the subject seemed too miserably personal.

He said that his first relationship was one in which the other person broke up with him because he, Interviewer Boy, wouldn't tell his super-Christian, Texas conservative family about his realization that he was not heterosexual.

"That's not fair," I said. "They didn't have to know, given their way of thinking."

"Right. They told me that I'm now damned to hell." He laughed.

"The hell is being such as you are in this world," I said.

"That's right!" he said. He laughed again.

The story continued. His parents, as to be expected, couldn't accept the news. His mother cried, he said. I couldn't bear to hear that. Why couldn't she go into another room to cry?

"Too bad you're not Rufus Wainwright," I said. "I bet his parents didn't cry."

"Isn't he great? Don't you love him?"

I said I did, ever since I'd seen him sing "My Funny Valentine" on the David Letterman Show, one of the few great musical acts ever on that show. Why? Who chooses the musical acts, was something I often wondered as I changed to the weather channel.

A twenty-seven-year-old boy had told me, about Rufus Wainwright, "He's gay." I was surprised. I used to love his mother's voice when she was one of the McGarrigle sisters in the nineteen-seventies and -eighties—and now this startling fact.

"Everyone knows it," the twenty-seven-year-old had said. "You can't have him."

"I meant I loved his performance. I don't fancy relationships with twenty-year-old boys," I said. "I'm still in love with Elvis Presley and President Kennedy. I think of Craig Ferguson and Paul McCartney in the boyfriend department."

BUT BACK to the bad thing. The bad thing was this: I asked how his weekend was, just to be polite. I hate weekends and can't imagine a good one. People are out all over the place, crowding things up. They're all doing different things at the same time, going here and there, every which way without any serious goals. That has always been too much for me and has been the cause of anxiety, and also of my method of doing errands on weeknights, as late as possible.

Then there are organized social activities—just as bad.

The answer to my question about the interviewer's weekend was "Horrible! I just had this horrendous breakup with this guy." He started to describe it in detail. It involved a middle-aged man and a Mexican teenager.

My favorite childhood books were *Heidi* and *The Secret Garden.* Since age five, my favorite movie had always been *The Red Shoes,* and now I was expected to listen to this.

"Oh, please, don't tell me," I said.

"Why? We're friends."

"Well, one, we just met, or just didn't meet. Two, my friends never tell each other this—even in college we didn't. We were discreet."

He persisted with this tale of the sordid triangular breakup as I begged him to stop.

"This is like the life of Tennessee Williams," I said. "You know, in our present times, you can have a real relationship, right out in the open."

"But it's new to me," he said. "I don't know how."

"Well, learn," I said. "Learn fast. Go back to that shrink you said you went to."

★ ★ ★

ONE NIGHT during a conversation about his neighborhood, in Austin, he said that there were all these great old houses from the twenties and thirties that were being torn down in order to build new ugly houses. The old houses were free to take away, and had all the great molding.

I said, "Why don't you take the old houses and move them and sell them?"

"I tried that," he said. "It was the worst experience of my life."

"Did you have a business partner with any experience?"

"Yeah, the guy tried to kill me once or twice."

"What? How?"

"He was an investor in the business plan. Things weren't going well. He tried to choke me and then tried to hit me with a claw hammer."

"What?" I said. I was laughing and so was he. "Why?" I asked.

"I just asked him, 'What's wrong with you today? Why are you acting like this?' He was in a bad mood."

"That was all?" I asked.

"We were losing money."

"That's business, right?"

"I'm not quite sure he hasn't already murdered one or two people."

"What?"

"He might have killed a man or two. I once heard him say, 'We're gonna take him fishing.' I think that means kill. When he tried to choke me—I'm not a big guy, but I'm younger, I'm strong—I escaped the chokehold. But when I ducked the hammer, he elbowed me in the face and busted my lip—it swelled all up. It was huge."

"How do you know people like this? What's his real job? In the gangster world?" I'm used to verbal assault only. I read the *National Enquirer* headlines for fun.

"No, he has an appliance repair business."

"Is this some gay thing?"

"No, he's married. He has kids. His wife hates me."

"It's a gay thing he doesn't want to face," I said. "You remind him of it."

"She hates me because he and I spent time together. He acted like a father."

"A father-gay thing? Oh, no," I said.

"Well, he liked to go to yard sales together Saturday mornings. He was always wheeling and dealing and doing business. We got to this house sale one time, and he found the house owner and asked, 'Do you have any guns?' The owner says, 'Yeah, I got guns.' Then the owner brings out the guns and they make a deal and he buys all the guns. He bought a 1941 Smith and Wesson rifle. The others were handguns."

"I can't believe this was your business partner. Guns? Right out on the front lawn?"

"Sure, guns. Everyone in Texas has guns. I have a gun."

"Why? Why can't you have pepper spray?"

"It's Texas. We have guns."

★ ★ ★

"So anyway we decide to move this house."

"Before or after the attempted murder?"

"Before, I think. I asked around for a house mover. Everyone is moving houses here. They tell me the mover I need to get is Del Junior Griffin. 'You've got to get Del Junior Griffin, he's the best house mover.'"

"Del Junior? Do people really have those names in Texas?" I said. "This is too good to be true."

"Yes, they're all, like, 'You have to get Del Junior. He's the one. He's the only one.' But, naturally, Del Junior was too busy to take it on. He was booked up for months, or years. I begged him because I'd already made the other financial arrangements for the lot and all. Finally, Del Junior Griffin told me, 'Get Sammy Sanchez.' And Sammy Sanchez is not the good one. He works with this other guy, PeeWee."

"It's like that book by William Faulkner. Someone is named Popeye."

"It is like that."

As the story continued, people had these names: Jimbo, Butch, Billy, Earl, Tubs. Those were the ones who lived in trailers. The last names were usually Jones or Smith. Then there were the illegal Mexican immigrants—Pedro Santos, Jimmy Gomez, Lucky Hernandez.

When he continued his story about the house mover, he

talked faster and in his southern accent. This made the story even more fun to hear. Not only is all the world a stage, but the phone is, too.

He said he'd made a deal with Sammy Sanchez. He'd paid him in advance—not just half—maybe all. I couldn't follow it. It was causing that special kind of anxiety—business-mistake anxiety. "I was just out of college. I didn't know anything."

"What about your fifty-year-old business partner?"

"Oh, he didn't know about it—I think. So it came time to move the house because it was going to be torn down imminently to build a Target."

"What's a target?" I pictured a gigantic shooting target for all those Texans and their guns.

"No, Target, the chain store. Don't you know that?"

"Where we live we don't have those things. That's why we live here."

"No Wal-Mart or Costco?"

"No, no, no." I remembered being told that a Kmart was allowed into a fake-colonial-style shopping center in the next town only after a long battle over prohibiting the store to sell guns. It was a true story.

"So, anyway, I was begging Sammy Sanchez week after week to please move the house. I'd call him. I told him how badly I had to get the house moved. He'd never call me back. I went to his trailer home and sat outside in my truck every day waiting for him. His wife would come out and say he wasn't there, but I saw him right through the plastic window. Finally, he'd come out and say, in this Texas drawl, 'Oh, it's *you*.'" He did an excellent low-life accent.

"What did they think of you?"

"Nothing. They called me 'College Boy.' They'd say"—he did the drawl—"'Oh, it's *you* again. It's College Boy.' I'd wait all day every day. It was so boring. I'd either be frantically calling my friends on my cell phone or reading Henry James."

"Which Henry James?"

"*The Turn of the Screw.*"

"Did you get the irony?"

"No, I was too crazed with fear. One day, he and his sons came out with rifles and started shooting into the air. They shot birds and things."

"Was that a hint?"

"Maybe. I wasn't any threat to them. And I was always polite. Oh, I forgot this! His seventeen-year-old son came out and told me how he and his father had gone to San Antonio and they'd both had sex with this black prostitute they'd picked up at a convenience store." Here he had to stop and laugh. "Can you believe that? How could they both have sex with the same prostitute?"

"It was convenient," I said.

He began to laugh harder. "Both of them with this one prostitute?" He couldn't stop laughing.

"A father-and-son kind of activity well suited for Texas."

"Suddenly all the electricity has gone off," he said. "What does it mean?"

HAPPY TRAILS TO YOU

"Power failure due to global warming and demand for air-conditioning."

"My dog is scared. Now I have to calm him down." I heard him talk to his dog in a way people talk to babies. He sounded so kind.

"Now I hear all these sirens," he said. "What could it be?"

"It's probably a terrorist attack," I said.

"Who would be so stupid to bomb a small town in Texas?"

"Bush," I said. "He's the main terrorist in the United States. Then he and Karl Rove will blame it on Iran."

"Really? Could it be?"

"Anything can be now, with those guys."

"Okay, well, if I die in a terrorist attack, would you please call my father—Don Davies, in Centerville, Texas—and tell him I wasn't really gay?"

This was one of the saddest last requests I'd ever heard, but I forged on.

"Of course. I'll tell him it was a phase—you were just thinking about it. You were never in a relationship."

"Great!" he said. He was laughing again.

"I'll tell him you were engaged to a lovely Christian girl."

He laughed more at that. Then he said, "Say she's a real WASP."

"Why? Why does he deserve that?"

"It's what he wishes for."

"Is he one?" I asked.

"No, he's just a Christian zealot."

"Well, too bad. I'm not telling him WASP. After all the misery he's caused you over the gay subject, this is a good enough compromise."

"Well, okay. It's probably not an attack anyway. The sirens have stopped. It's getting hot in here without the air conditioner. How will I sleep and go to work tomorrow?" He had a real job selling land.

"This happened to us once. I ordered twelve battery-powered fans from a marine store where they keep them for people's steamy boats."

"You're so crazy!" he said, laughing in his fun way. "I'll be fine. But my dog is still scared."

During all this time of imagining the wretched night without air-conditioning, I couldn't get off my mind what he wanted me to tell his father. It really was the saddest last request I'd ever heard. I'd never heard any, when I thought about it.

I was serious about the terrorist attack, which we all know is imminent. We were laughing about the call to his father, but he was serious.

"Could I write to him instead?" I asked. "I don't think I could talk on the phone to him. It would be like talking to Cheney."

"Not that bad!"

"He's a Republican-conservative-Christian zealot, isn't he?"

"Yes, my whole family."

"You said that they hold hands and pray in public, in restaurants."

"Yes," he laughed.

"They have guns."

"Yes, everyone has guns here."

"Why don't you visit Paris?"

"My aunt wants to take me."

"Go," I said. "Go to Paris. Go to Rome. Get out of Texas."

I was beginning to have a better understanding of how things had gotten to be the way they were in the world.

AFTER THE interviewer had been kicked out of his family, and had been abandoned by the boyfriend who made him tell them his secret, he was in a bad state. Alone, all alone. He had many friends of various persuasions, but they couldn't help him. He thought about suicide. He had found a shrink, he said, and the doctor had helped him. He recovered after several years.

"Did the shrink mention the chain-smoking?" I asked.

"No, he didn't care about that."

"He should care. All these things go together. What about the Snickers and the Little Debbies?"

"No, he didn't talk about my nutritional problems, or smoking."

"All shrinks are bad now," I said. "The great ones are gone."

"No, he helped me. I'm almost back to normal." He took a deep inhale.

One rule I tried to enforce was no smoking during talking.

He couldn't agree. He was a serious addict. Those poisoned inhales were distracting.

"Didn't it occur to you that you shouldn't be associated with those people?"

"I was so young. I was in too deep. It was my business, too. I did it to make a living. My partner, the one who tried to choke me, was demanding cash."

"Couldn't you do something else?"

"It was too late. So this guy Sammy Sanchez finally agrees to move the house and gets his crew ready. It's the middle of the night, like two a.m., and I met him at the house. He's there with these drunken, drugged-up guys—they take three chain saws and saw off the roof. I asked, 'Is that a good idea?' They ignored me. I was no one to them. So they get the house onto these beams and start pulling it with a Mack truck, without the roof, through the streets."

"Don't you need permits and things for that?"

"They paid off some policeman to accompany them to make it look legal."

"You mean you can just do anything in Texas? Aren't there any laws?"

"None that can't be broken. Anyway, they didn't make any provisions for turning off the power, so this one guy is standing up, holding a board up high from the inside of the roofless house, pushing up the power lines, smacking them, smashing

trees, and the house siding is bowed and flying off everywhere!
I was following in my truck. When they stopped to bounce some
cars off the road, I saw this one guy under the house smoking
dope and using a blowtorch at the same time! I was panicked. I
was crazed with anxiety. I smoked two packs of Camels."

"What does bounce mean?" I asked.

"One guy pounds on the hood of the cars, one pounds the
trunk, one pounds the door, and the car jumps off the street
right onto the lawns. This is a middle-class neighborhood, but
old, without garages. The neighborhood people are outside in
their bathrobes screaming at us. They had lost power for their
air-conditioning. These drunken guys tore down trees, power
lines, everything, and just kept going."

"How could this go on in the middle of the night, and no
law-enforcement officials intervene?"

"Laws aren't enforced in Texas. I told you."

"This must be how they killed Kennedy."

"Yes," he said. He didn't care about that. He hadn't even been
born yet. I had to face that about people every day. They hadn't
been born in 1963, or they were one year old.

"Finally, they arrive at the destination, the lot for the house,
and they back it onto the lot crooked. It's facing the neighbor's
house instead of the street. Then they're ready to leave. They
drank some whiskey and took some pills and dope and then I
left. I was too freaked.

"I begged Sammy Sanchez to straighten out the house and
get it off the beams and he promised he would the next day or

week. But the house just sat there, crooked, without a roof, day after day. I had to find him. He had lived in a trailer, but he was evicted. I had to drive all around outside Austin, to this town where he was living in an extended-stay hotel."

"What's that?" I asked.

"You know—you live there longer, cheaper. They're really sleazy."

I was afraid that if I told him the only hotel I'd stayed in for a couple of weeks was the old Ritz-Carlton in Boston, he'd ask, "What's that?"

I'd have to explain, "It's a landmark in Beacon Hill, near where Robert Lowell lived. But it wasn't called extended-stay." He might ask, "Who's Robert Lowell?"

"I think Sammy Sanchez once said he'd start the job. He took me to lunch at Hooters and paid for it. I think he was just trying to get more money from me."

"Hooters? Do they have food?"

"What did you think?"

"I thought beer, waitresses in lewd uniforms, and fried wings of things."

"No, it's just a junky place like TGIF or Bennigan's. Don't you have those up there in Yankee world? They're all over Texas. They have fake trophies and crap all over the walls. They all look alike. The food is all fried junk."

I told Interview Boy he had begun to remind me of someone—someone innocent and naïve, and everyone takes advantage of this person.

"Who is it?" I asked him. "It's either Ed Grimley or David Copperfield. Or Candide or Tiny Tim or his father."

"Bob Cratchit? Oh, yes. It's true. You know, I was always chosen to play Tiny Tim in the Christmas pageant because of my small stature."

"And your other qualities—like Christian goodness, optimism, innocence, happiness—not knowing anything bad is about to happen."

"Yeah, that's me. So the house sat crooked. People were after me. I was terrified I'd be sued and I had no money left. I had to go around the neighborhood and personally apologize to everyone. I had to pay them off."

"You mean money?"

"No, like cartons of cigarettes. That's what they like. Then this other guy tracks me down and says, 'Hey, these are my beams. Sammy Sanchez stole them from me and I'm taking them back.'

"'Listen, I don't want your beams,' I said. 'Sammy's supposed to build this foundation and give back the beams.' But the guy said he needed the beams soon, like right away. These guys are always stealing each other's beams because house moving is a big business here.

"So, the next day I went to look at the house. It was still on the beams, and there I see Del Junior Griffin drive up in his truck. I said, 'Oh, thank you. You came to help. Thank you so much.'

"He just looked at the house and laughed. He said, 'No, I heard about it. I just came to have a look at it for myself.' Then he laughed some more and left."

"Why do you live in Texas again?" I asked. I never liked it. Even in grade school, I couldn't learn the states because that one state was so large and badly shaped. It startled me out of concentrating on the others.

"You know, I think I heard that Texas is the only state with a bar in the state Capitol building. You can actually buy drinks. Or maybe it's right next to the Capitol. My friends told me they go to a gym nearby and the legislators come from work on the Senate floor and they're drunk. They're at the gym drunk, too. To and fro, drunk."

"I believe that, but it is unbelievable."

"So now it's not just Texas, it's Washington. It's the government. A bunch of drunken bums."

"With guns."

"That's right—with guns. That's how we got where we are now. Anyway, I heard about this guy who might get the house off the beams. I called him—his wife said he was in jail. I asked what for and she said, 'Arson.' Then this other guy I heard about, Duane, or something, he couldn't do it. His wife said his truck had been burned down. A lightbulb went on in my head. I asked, 'Was it burned down by Butch?' And she said, 'Yes.' So one guy I needed was in prison for burning the truck, and the other guy was the one whose truck had been burned." We both started laughing in a hysterical way.

"So Sammy Sanchez never came. One night, there was a big thunderstorm. I panicked. I went late at night to Home Depot and bought a bunch of tarps and bungee cords and drove to the house. I climbed up to the top and tried to tie on the tarps with the bungee cords. I was up there forever."

"All alone?"

"Yes, alone. But the wind was blowing and it was raining hard. So I finally couldn't get the tarps to stay on. I sat there on top of the house and cried. I just sat in the rain on the tarped section and cried for a long time. Then I gave up. I got into my truck and smoked some Camels and went home."

"The smoking could be the worst part," I said.

"Well, I plan to stop. I'm going to stop even though I love smoking more than anything in the whole world."

"It's such a sad story," I said.

ONE NIGHT when we were talking, he said, "You know what I like about your work? It's kind of a trail."

"But it's not a happy trail," I said. "Do you know that song?"

"Of course. Here, I'll find it." He got his computer and found a tinkly electronic, wordless version. I asked him to keep going until he found the real thing. Then he sang a bit of it: "'Happy trails to you, until we meet again.' Roy Rogers and Dale Evans. Did you like them?"

"No, I wasn't interested in cowboys and Westerns," I said. "But I liked the song. I wanted cowgirl boots, and my mother bought them at B. Altman, a once great, now defunct department store."

The boots were too small for my long feet, and she insisted

on returning them although I was pleading and begging. I also wanted pink ballet pointe shoes, but the children's sizes at ballet class weren't long enough. She said antibiotics like aureomycin had caused our feet to grow too fast. Later on, she read *Silent Spring,* just like Al Gore's mother. She was proven right.

The interviewer wasn't interested in this. As he fiddled with his computer, Googling here and there and everywhere, he started reading two lines from a poem. The poem had the words "golden chances."

"I always think about that," I said. "It's from some musical: 'I let my golden chances pass me by.'"

"Why do you think of that?" he asked.

"Because that's how I feel. I didn't know other people felt the same way."

"What musical?" He was back onto his computer immediately.

"Something like *Oklahoma!* Do you know what that is?"

"Of course. I'm not a complete dunce. Except in some ways."

"The song might be 'If I Loved You.'"

"Okay, here it is—from *Carousel,*" he said.

"That's it. I just saw it in a documentary—a duet with Shirley Jones and who? John Raitt?"

"Here—Gordon MacRae. I'll play it on iTunes. Is this the one?"

An electronic version without words came over the phone.

"No," I said. "The real song."

He kept going, playing one after another. There was no re-semblance to the song.

"There. This must be it," he said.

Finally, I heard those lines.

"Can you find 'Oklahoma!'—the one with Bonnie Raitt's father?"

"Who's he?"

"John Raitt. He had a perfect voice for the song." I figured Interview Boy would know him only if I said Bonnie Raitt first. I was right.

WHENEVER I saw John Raitt sing the song "Oh, What a Beautiful Morning," I remembered my father walking around the house singing the same song. He had a deep voice, too.

One morning, when I was about five, I woke up and saw him choosing a tie from his closet. The closet was in the hallway in front of my room. I was still in bed and this was my view: my father tying his tie and singing, "Oh, what a beautiful morning, Oh, what a beautiful day."

I thought about my father and his morning. How could it be beautiful? He'd ride the subway to Manhattan, work in an office all day, come home on the subway, and the beautiful day would be over. No blue skies or high corn for him, but still singing that song as he tied his tie. An upstanding fellow. I had an inkling even then.

Two other songs he might start to sing in the afternoon on

weekends were "Oklahoma!" and "The Surrey with the Fringe on Top." After he and my mother had seen *South Pacific*, he'd sing a few lines from "Some Enchanted Evening." Just like that, out of nowhere, I'd hear the song.

They were always going to Rodgers and Hammerstein musicals. My mother would escape from us, her annoying children, and meet him in Manhattan. She'd wear an elegant black dress, black high-heeled shoes, and even a little black beaded hat. The next day, she'd tell us about the musical, and my father, at some point during the day, would start singing one of the songs.

It never occurred to me to ask to see a Broadway musical. I figured they were for grown-ups, or that's what she told me, and I believed it. They'd buy the albums and we'd all listen to the songs. But my father singing them out of nowhere was even better. I didn't expect him to be able to sing like that.

Since I found the stories, dialogue, and acting to be fake and idiotic, I had the idea that musicals were a waste of time, other than the music. I never mentioned this, because that's what most entertainment was like in the nineteen-fifties until Elvis Presley and rock and roll changed everything.

I'd heard people say the world was completely different before the automobile and after. I thought that went for rock and roll, too.

I told Interview Boy a bit of this, but he wasn't paying much attention. He had no interest in history of any kind. He'd gotten his own idea.

"Hey, these would make great titles for porn films!" he said. Then he began reading them off.

"'When the Children Are Asleep.'" He started laughing. "'You'll Never Walk Alone.'" In between each title, he kept laughing more happily. I started laughing, too, because it was so ludicrous.

"Look, you can't deny this," he said. "'You're a Queer One, Julie Jordan.'"

"'If I Loved You'?" I said. "No one could think the way you do unless they were trying too hard. You're like Freud."

"I'm just like him."

"You have a one-track mind for homoeroticism."

As he read on, we both became hysterical and couldn't stop laughing.

"Wait, look at *Oklahoma!*," he said. "'I Can't Say No,' 'People Will Say We're in Love.'"

Laughing is supposed to be good for the health, but it felt as if some valve might burst and I might die. I had to get up to do Dr. Weil's breathing exercises.

"Wait, listen to *Seven Brides for Seven Brothers*," he said. "'Queen of the May'! These are so perfect for porn titles! Look at *The King and I*—'We Kiss in a Shadow,' 'Shall We Dance?'"

"'Shall We Dance?' was my mother's favorite song from the show."

"*South Pacific*," he said, still laughing even more. "'Some Enchanted Evening'! 'A Wonderful Guy'!"

"Those too," I said. "She loved them."

I was thinking about my parents again and how much my mother had loved the song "If I Loved You." And I was thinking of my father and our first house. That house had a floor with a dark-green linoleum center and a black-and-white-striped border. Our next house had Oriental rugs and a stereo for those albums. I was wishing I could be back there with my parents. I wanted to talk to them.

I sometimes wondered about John Raitt and his daughter, Bonnie Raitt. When he was up high on that horse singing in that great, deep voice, then going home, maybe thinking about a name for a baby—Bonnie, or what other names they considered—never did it cross his mind how Bonnie would grow up. Her singing career; the time she said to David Letterman, "My songs are my children"; the white streak in her long red hair; her stories of being on the road with her music "guys." These are things John Raitt could not have fathomed.

As I was listening to Interview Boy and laughing—the memory of the beautiful mornings and days and songs of my family besmirched—I saw that laughing was a form of crying. It must have been physiologically related. People said they laughed until they cried. It was true.

I wondered how I'd gone from that beautiful morning in childhood to this kind of middle-of-night morning, listening to jokes about those song titles this way.

How did it happen? If I thought about it for the rest of my life, and researched it as history, like Spengler's *The Decline of the West* or Gibbon's *Decline and Fall of the Roman Empire*, or as psychiatry, like Freud's case studies of Anna O. or Dora or the Wolf Man or even the Rat Man, I might understand the whole story.

The best would be to live it all over, from the beginning. This time I could do it right.

ACKNOWLEDGMENTS

The author wishes to thank the John Simon Guggenheim
Foundation for supporting her work.

She also thanks L.M., J.K., P.H.S., Mrs. J.W., M.N., and A.T.
for their help.

The author is especially grateful to Macy Halford
for all her work on the preparation of this book.

She is also grateful to Dr. Kurt Eissler, 1908–1999,
for his wisdom and kindness.

ABOUT THE AUTHOR

JULIE HECHT is the author of *Do the Windows Open?, Was This Man a Genius?: Talks with Andy Kaufman,* and *The Unprofessionals.* Her stories have been published in *The New Yorker* and *Harper's* and in anthologies. She has won an O. Henry Prize and received a Guggenheim Fellowship. She lives on the east end of Long Island in winter and in Massachusetts in summer and fall.

Printed in the United States
By Bookmasters